THE BEAST

"Riotously silly and asks all the important
questions. Where DO all the hairbands go?"
Louie Stowell, bestselling author of *Loki*

"Garlic baguettes and girl power – what's not to
love! Absolutely bonkers and so much fun!"
Ellie Taylor, comedian, actor, author, presenter

"Monstrously brilliant fun. We love Knobbly Bottom!"
**Matt Coyne, comedian and bestselling
author of *Man vs Baby***

"So funny... I LOVE IT!"
**Alex Milway, bestselling author of
Hotel Flamingo and *Big Sky Mountain***

"Brilliantly original and laugh-out-loud hilarious...
[an] explosive and entertaining debut"
**Tamsin Winter, award-winning author of
Being Miss Nobody, Jemima Small and *Girl, In Real Life***

"Witty, twisty-turny and laugh-a-minute..."
**Jules Howard, zoological correspondent,
science-writer and author**

About the Author

Emily-Jane Clark is an author, drama teacher and TV comedy writer. Her work has been featured on *The Mash Report*, *The Jonathan Ross Show* and *Mock the Week*. Her book for adults, *Sleep is for the Weak* – a humorous antithesis to baby sleep advice – was an Amazon bestseller.

Before turning her hand to writing, she was a failed pop star, holiday-park entertainer and a gherkin-putter-inner at McDonald's. She then went on to be a journalist, but there weren't enough opportunities for bum jokes, so she decided to write comedy instead.

She was also a finalist in the Funny Women awards and winner of a very hard pub quiz, and once got hit by a bus.

Emily-Jane lives in a village in the East Midlands with her two daughters where she writes books, scripts, angry poems and endless to-do lists.

You can find her at www.emilyjaneclark.com, on X @EmilyJaneClark or on Instagram @emilyjane.clark

EMILY-JANE CLARK

The BEASTS of
KNOBBLY
BOTTOM

RISE OF THE ZOMBIE PIGS

ILLUSTRATED BY
JEFF CROWTHER

SCHOLASTIC

Published in the UK by Scholastic, 2024
1 London Bridge, London, SE1 9BG
Scholastic Ireland, 89E Lagan Road,
Dublin Industrial Estate, Glasnevin, Dublin, D11 HP5F

Text © Emily-Jane Clark, 2024
Illustrations by Jeff Crowther © Scholastic, 2024

The right of Emily-Jane Clark to be identified as the author of this work has been
asserted by them under the Copyright, Designs and Patents Act 1988.

ISBN 978 0702 32511 3

A CIP catalogue record for this book
is available from the British Library.

Printed in Great Britain by Clays Ltd, Elcograf S.p.A.
Paper made from wood grown in sustainable forests
and other controlled sources.

1 3 5 7 9 10 8 6 4 2

www.scholastic.co.uk

For my parents – Madeline and Jim,
who always believed in my knobbly bottom

CONTENTS

CHAPTER ONE

The scariest thing ever that started with CAKE

My name is Maggie McKay, and the scariest thing that has EVER happened to me started with a delicious chocolate cake.

I know what you're thinking. *"Nothing scary ever starts with chocolate cake, Maggie."* Only nice things happen when cakes are around – like birthdays or *The Great British Bake Off* or National Eat Cake for Breakfast Day (when I invent it). Well, I would have thought *exactly* the same before **The Scariest Thing That Ever Happened** happened. Now I'm not sure I'll be able to enjoy cake ever again. That's how scary it was. Luckily, because I am a super-brave beast hunter now, I lived to tell the whole terrifying tale. This tale.

So if you like terrifying tales, carry on reading this book. BUT if you don't like them then maybe go and read something about kittens and candy floss instead. (Although, do **NOT** read a book about kittens that have EATEN candy floss because my friend Rav's cat once ate a whole bag of the stuff and started running into walls and hissing at us with **PINK SPIT**, which *was* actually terrifying.)

Still reading? Fine, then I'll tell you **EVERYTHING**. But don't say I didn't warn you.

My story begins on a lovely sunny summer's day. Which is a bit disappointing because this is the sort of story that should start with a creepy old storm or something. But annoyingly the jolly old sun was shining on **Knobbly Bottom**, making it a very *unscary* day.

I should explain that the sun was not shining on a bum with knobbly bits on it, but on the village of **Knobbly Bottom**, where I live with my mum, Lucy, my little sister, Lily, and my three pet stones, Emmaline, Madeline and Vaseline. We moved here from a flat in Leicester at the beginning of the summer, which I was **NOT** happy about until I found out that **Knobbly Bottom** is the WEIRDEST and most EXCITING place to live in the country (maybe even the world)!

We live in a small cottage on the village green with a big garden that doesn't have any pets in it because my mum won't let me have one. In fact, there's something you should know about my mum. She loves NOT letting me have stuff. It is her favourite hobby.

THINGS MY MUM WON'T
LET ME HAVE

1. A pet
2. A horse
3. A mobile phone
4. A centipede farm (like an ant farm but for centipedes because they are much cooler)
5. A swimming pool
6. Grapes that are not cut in half
7. A robot cleaner (to tidy my room)
8. Bubblegum
9. A big sword

So imagine my **SHOCK** on this lovely summer's day in **Knobbly Bottom** when my mum went and said YES to something! She said if me and Lily "played nicely" (by the way, when my mum says "play nicely" she actually means "play in silence and don't ask for any snacks") while she did some work on her computer, then YES we *could* have **CAKE** in the garden.

Later that afternoon, she told me and Lily to come outside, and there on the patio table was the **BIGGEST CHOCOLATE CAKE** I had ever seen, looking all delicious and pleased with itself.

"Ta-dah!" She smiled, pointing at the huge cake. "Fresh from the supermarket delivery van this morning. I'll go and grab some plates and cutlery!"

And that was when me and Lily made the mistake of being KIND. The cake was so big and delicious-looking we thought we would ask our friend Fred, who lives next door with his granddad, if he wanted to share it with us. So we climbed over the little fence into Fred's garden (and before you tell me off for climbing over people's fences, Fred's granddad, Mr Tibble, said we could come over and play *whenever* we wanted, so there) and banged on the door of a big wooden shed at the end of the garden that had this sign on it:

FRED'S SHED– KEEP OUT

JUST A NORMAL SHED
FULL OF BORING SHEDDY THINGS
AND MASSIVE SPIDERS
AND RATS THAT BITE
NOTHING TO SEE HERE SO BE ON YOUR WAY

"What's the password?" yelled a voice from inside the shed. "Tenth rule of army training: always have a password."

One thing you should know about Fred is that his dad is in the army, so Fred thinks he knows *everything* about it.

"But you haven't even told us the password, Fred," I said, trying the handle, only to find it was locked.

"That's exactly what an enemy would say," Fred's voice replied.

"I am not an enemy. I'm a Maggie and you know it!"

"Ah, that's exactly what an enemy *pretending* to be a Maggie would say!" said Fred.

"How are we supposed to know the password if you haven't told us the password?" I said, beginning to regret my decision to come and get him.

"We've got cake, Fred!" yelled Lily, and finally Fred burst out of the shed holding two forks.

"Sponge, fruit, red velvet, chiffon or chocolate?" he asked. "I need to know which type of fork to bring."

Another thing you should know about Fred is that his dad is a *chef* in the army, so he knows LOADS about things like cakes, spatulas, cooking and forks.

"Bring both!" I said, and we raced back to our garden.

I should explain that Fred's shed wasn't *actually* filled with boring sheddy things or massive spiders or bitey rats. We cleverly made that sign to stop people going inside and discovering that it was not actually a shed at all but a … **TOP-SECRET BEAST HUNTER HEADQUARTERS (BHHQ)**.

After a battle with an army of **VAMPIRE SHEEP** earlier in the summer, we decided it would be sensible to have a place to (1) make cunning plans, (2) store our beast-hunting kit (mostly pans, water guns, spatulas and garlic), and (3) keep a stash of emergency Jaffa cakes for when we were bored.

Now, if you're the kind of rebel who NEVER reads the first book in a series, then you must be thinking, *"What the heckedy-doo-dah with knobs on are vampire sheep?"* Well, I'm afraid I'm far too busy telling you *this* story to go into that right now, so you'll just have to blimming well read it. All I will say is that **Knobbly Bottom** is built on top of an ancient underground city called **Beastopia**, which was once home to horrible things like BEASTS and BAD MAGIC and BOGEYS. The GOOD news is that the nasty creatures who lived there were conquered long, long ago, and the gateway to the city is now safely sealed. Well, when I say "safely sealed", there is also some bad news. Sometimes leftover bad **Beastopian** magic sneaks up into the village like a rascal and makes terrible things happen ... like turning innocent sheep into **vampires** and maybe making innocent chocolate cakes **DISAPPEAR FROM PATIO TABLES!**

Yes, that's right. When we got back to our garden with Fred's forks at the ready, that delicious cake was completely and utterly GONE.

"Where's the cake?" cried Lily, staring at the empty plate on the table.

I picked up the plate to examine it and popped

one of the few remaining delicious crumbs
into my mouth just as my mum came outside
with a knife.

She stared at the empty plate in my hand in **SHOCK**. "Have you eaten the *whole* cake, Maggie?" she said.

It was so unfair! You accidentally eat half your little sister's birthday cake **ONE** time when you were six years old and you are forever known as the family food thief!

"It wasn't me!" I told her. "We went to get Fred and when we came back it was gone!"

Mum did NOT look convinced. "Cakes don't just disappear into thin air!" she said.

"Well, this one did!" I said, folding my arms. "Tell her, Lily!"

"I didn't see it disappear," said Lily.

"You can't see things that disappear, Lily!" I huffed. "That's the whole point!"

"Maybe somebody stole it?" suggested Fred.

"We've been cake-burgled!" I said. "Mum, call the police!"

But can you believe my mum would NOT call the police? She said police officers do not investigate missing cakes. Especially ones that *might* have disappeared into children's tummies.

In fact, she was *so* determined not to call the police that I said maybe *she* ate the cake herself and this was all a big cover-up. Why else wouldn't she want us to find out what happened?

"Don't be silly, Maggie!" she said. "If I wanted to eat a whole cake, I would have just bought myself one and eaten it, not promised some to you and Lily, then wolfed it down when you weren't looking."

That was a good point. In fact, I don't understand why my mum isn't *always* eating cake. When I grow up, I'm definitely going to eat cake all day, every day, AND have five hundred pets AND never clean my teeth again. Imagine being allowed to do **ANYTHING** you want and still *choosing* to do boring stuff like eat vegetables and tidy the kitchen every single day! Grown-ups are so weird.

"Maybe it was GREEDY MICE!" said Lily. "Mice love cakes."

"Don't be silly, Lily," I replied. "Mice would not be able to eat that big cake with their teeny tiny mouths!"

"Well, I will NOT be buying any more cakes for a very long time!" Mum tutted and picked up the empty plate. "I wouldn't want any 'mice' eating them all up!"

Then she stomped off back into the house, leaving us staring at the sad, cakeless patio table.

Now, you are probably enjoying thinking about some cute little mice gobbling up chocolate treats with their tiny mouths, BUT I'm sorry to tell you that something much **scarier** than that had happened to our cake.

We just didn't know it yet...

CHAPTER TWO

The cake-burglar strikes again

The next day it was *uncreepily* sunny again. In fact, it was so sunny that a man on the news called it a "heatwave" and said that even TRAINS were too hot to move. But can you believe that my mum told us that WE had to move because we were going on a picnic? But there is one thing you should know about my mum's picnics. They are totally rubbish. Especially when there is no leftover chocolate cake to go in them.

MY MUM'S BORESOME PICNIC

1. Smelly tuna sandwiches with the crusts still on – GROSS
2. A packet of digestives aka the most boring biscuits EVER

3. Bananas – EVIL
4. Apples – BORING
5. Raisins – POINTLESS
6. Bottle of cold water and **NOT** Coke because apparently stuff that tastes nice is bad for us

But I quite like going to the park and my mum said we could have a blue ice pole to eat on the way.

As soon as we got there, me and Lily went off to play while my mum laid out all the food on a big blanket.

But the thing about playing with Lily is this: she is really BAD at taking turns.

"Mummy!" she cried from the top of the slide a few minutes later. "Maggie won't play with me."

This was a total lie. I HAD been playing with Lily, but it turned out that "slide superheroes" was just watching her go down the slide on her tummy while shouting, **"SUPER LILY TO THE RESCUE!"** That was literally the whole game.

"Maggie, play with your sister, please!" shouted Mum.

"But she won't let me have a turn on the slide!" I shouted back.

"I know! How about we play hide-and-seek?" said my mum, who had just sat down and poured herself a big coffee from her flask. "You two hide and I'll count to ten!"

By the way, when my mum says, "I'll count to ten," she actually means: "I'll count for as long as it takes to drink my coffee, THEN I'll come and find you." But the joke is on her because it just gives me more time to find a brilliant hiding place!

"OK, but no peeping!" I told her, running off into the trees.

★

Mum found Lily straight away because she was just sitting at the bottom of the slide with her hands in front of her face (she is rubbish at hiding).

So then they both decided to search for me together. But it took them ages because I am **BRILLIANTASTIC** at hide-and-seek!

(In case you are wondering, I was under a bush that was the same colour green as my top – genius!)

But on *this* particular day it was a bad thing that I was so good at hiding, because if my mum had found me sooner, the CAKE THIEF might not have had a chance to strike again! *Eventually* they found me, and we went back to the blanket – only to find that THE FOOD HAD ALL GONE. Even the smelly sandwiches and the pointless raisins! And I BET you can guess who got the blame.

"Did you sneak back here and eat the picnic, Maggie?" said my mum, looking very confused.

"NO!" I said. "I don't even like tuna sandwiches or boring fruit!"

"That is true," she admitted, frowning and putting the plastic picnic plates back in the bag. "There must be some very hungry mice around the village at the moment. These things happen in the countryside because of all the wildlife.

It's completely normal."

But *then* I reminded her that **Knobbly Bottom** was NOT completely normal because normal places do NOT get taken over by evil **vampire sheep**.

"How many times do I have to tell you?" my mum said firmly. "Animals sometimes get poorly, and it can make them act strangely – like mad cow disease and swine flu."

"Or evilitus!" I said.

This is probably a good time to tell you that even though she *saw them with her own eyes*, my mum had decided she did NOT believe the sheep we'd defeated were vampires. Instead, her **Perfectly Logical Explanation** for the red-eyed scary beasts that had tried to take over the village was that they had "come down with something". She *even* tried to tell me that the reason our anti-vampire juice (three parts garlic, one part freshly blessed holy water) "cured" them was because garlic is full of "immune-system-boosting vitamins" that must have made them feel better.

The thing is, *she* never actually heard those nasty woolbags TALK like we did.

"I'm hungry!" whined Lily.

"Why don't we go to the shop and get something else for lunch?" said Mum, taking Lily's hand.

By the way, if you ever go to **Knobbly Bottom**, do not, I repeat, do NOT go to the village shop. Mostly because it is rubbish, hardly has any sweets and smells a bit like cabbage. But also because in the storeroom at the back lies the **Gateway to Beastopia** – aka the old underground city of evil where the bad magic lives...

And then there's **Gary the Great and Evil Child-Eater**, the strange old shopkeeper and Guardian of the Gateway. He would definitely give you a scare. But I suppose I should tell you before you FREAK OUT and call the police that Gary is not evil or great and he doesn't really eat children. He's actually a vegan. He just uses that name to try to stop children coming near the gateway. (He also doesn't want them in his shop anyway because he says they're too noisy. He may not be evil, but he *is* grumpy – although he did help us defeat the army of evil **vampire sheep**, so he's not all bad.)

"Hello, Gary!" My mum smiled as we walked into the shop. "We're after a little something for lunch. We think some greedy mice ate our picnic while we weren't looking!"

"Who do you thinks I am, Mr Starbuckles?" he groaned. Gary likes groaning. "All I gots is tins, butter, pickled critters, hornet's spit, slimeballs or a packet of hot cross buns."

"Ha! You are funny, Gary! We'll take the hot cross buns,

please! Do you want to go and fetch them, Maggie?" said my mum.

Now, **I LOVE hot cross buns**, so I made my way to the bakery shelf feeling very excited. BUT just as I was about to reach for the very last packet, a pair of greedy hands barged me out of the way and grabbed them first!

I turned round to see that the hands belonged to a girl of about my age. She wore blue dungarees, muddy wellies and had her red hair in two short curly pigtails (that actually did look like pigs' tails). And she was holding **MY** hot cross buns and looking very pleased with herself.

"I just love hot cross buns, don't you?" She smiled, smugly hugging the buns to her chest.

"Yes! That's why *I* was about to pick those up!" I said, folding my arms to show that I meant business.

"Oh dear. I hope you're not too CROSS about it! Hahahaha!" She laughed a horrible, loud, snorty laugh like a pig being tickled with a feather and walked over to the counter.

"I'll take these too," she said, lugging TWO big bags of potatoes and **SIXTEEN** packets of crisps on to the counter and handing Gary some money. *What a flipping greedy guts!*

"Enjoy your hot cross 'nones'!" she whispered to me as she left the shop with her two massive bags of food.

"She took our hot cross buns!" I said.

"Well, technically they weren't ours," my mum said. "She just got there first!"

"Only because she shoved me out of the way!" I pointed out.

"That be Celery Snoot," said Gary. "Her family own the big old pig farm in the village."

"She looked about your age, Maggie!" said Mum. "Let's invite her over for tea! It'll be nice for you to make friends before you start school."

By the way, my mum is **OBSESSED** with me starting school in September. Even though I told her that I'm a beast-hunting hero now and I have more important things to do than go to silly old Knobbly Bottom Primary School, she is still making me go. It's so unfair! If you ask me, it would be WAY more useful to stay at home and learn sword-fighting and kung fu off YouTube. And there was no way in a **SQUIZILLION** years I would make friends with a greedy bun stealer like **Celery Snoot**.

Anyway, Mum asked Gary if he had any more hot cross buns in the back, and he said something that made me forget all about Celery.

"I gots no more hot cross buns," said Gary. "I had a delivery from the bakers go missing from my doorstep last night. I went inside to get me basket and when I came back out, everything was a goner."

"Maybe it was the same greedy mice who ate our picnic!" said Mum, heading down to the tin aisle to find something else for lunch.

First the CAKE, then our PICNIC and now Gary's HOT CROSS BUNS?

"Gary," I whispered. "Could all this missing food have something to do with the bad magic? Should we call Nan Helsing?"

Nan Helsing is the local beast hunter. Yes, that's right – I live in a village that has its very own **BEAST HUNTER**. I told you **Knobbly Bottom** was WEIRD.

One thing you should know about Nan Helsing is this: she looks like a normal little old lady, but she has the skills of a superhero. She comes from a long line of beast hunters who have kept **Knobbly Bottom** safe from **Beastopian** evil for centuries.

BUT there was one big problem. Nan Helsing was away in Spain because she said she needed to "recharge her batteroids".

"I'll not be bothering Nan Helsing on her holidays abouts a few hungry mice," said Gary. "If the bad magic were back, methinks it'd be doing a lot worse than snaffling a few buns, don't you? And anyway, the gateway back there is safely secured under my VERY HEAVY freezer, thank you very much. Now skidaddle, skiddiwinks. I'm rushed off my feets here."

This was NOT true because we were the *only* people in the shop! Told you he was grumpy!

Gary and my mum might believe the missing

food was down to a few hungry mice, but I did NOT. Something strange was going on in **Knobbly Bottom**, I just knew it!

There was only one thing for it. I would have to call an URGENT SECRET SHED MEETING.

CHAPTER THREE

Courgettes and chaos

When we got home, Mum said she had made us some "Not Cross Buns", which turned out to be tuna sandwiches. She thought this was hilarious. Another thing you should know about my mum is that she is rubbish at jokes. And they are even WORSE when you are hungry.

Last week I said, "I'm hungry," and she said, "Hi, Hungry – I'm Lucy." So then I said, "No, I'm *really* hungry," and she said, "I'm *really* Lucy," and this went on and on and on. It was really annoying – especially because all I had eaten that day was breakfast, lunch, three chocolate biscuits, a yoghurt and a banana so I was *starving*.

Then another time I asked her if we could get a pizza for dinner, and she just kept saying,

"A piece o' what? A piece o' cabbage? A piece o' cheese? A piece o' my mind?" even though she knew jolly well what I meant.

Anyway, after I had *finally* eaten lunch, I went to tell Fred we needed an **URGENT SECRET SHED MEETING.**

But GUESS what! When I opened the front door, Fred was already there on my doorstep in FULL camouflage clothes with two spatulas tucked into his belt. I knew that Fred always carried a spatula in case of emergency, so TWO must mean a double emergency!

"I need to call an urgent secret shed meeting," said an out-of-breath Fred. "I think the…"

"BAD MAGIC IS BACK!" we both said at the same time.

★

Five minutes later, me and Fred were inside his shed – aka **Beast Hunter Headquarters** – sitting on two big beanbags. There was a massive whiteboard on the wall (for

31

plan-making, evidence notes and drawing pictures of poo with funny faces) and crates of army-edition kitchen utensils. We also had a notebook, two cartons of juice and a packet of emergency Jaffa cakes – which we opened straight away because it was *officially* an emergency. According to Fred, the chocolate cake, the picnic and Gary's hot cross buns were not the ONLY food that had gone missing in **Knobbly Bottom**.

He told me to PREPARE MYSELF FOR A SHOCK because what I was about to see was total grotbags. I took a deep breath, and he started riffling through the massive rucksack in the corner of the shed.

"Aha!" he said, holding up a sandwich bag full of something green and slimy!

"Ugh! What's that?" I groaned as he waved it in front of my face.

"A sandwich bag. Eleventh rule of army training: always carry sealable sandwich bags for

leftovers *and* gathering evidence,"
he said proudly.

"I mean what's *inside* the bag, Fred?" I asked,
squinting at the green squidgy clump.

"About two thirds of a courgette."

Then Fred told me that his granddad, Mr
Tibble, went to water his vegetable patch
this morning only to find every single one
of his prize-winning courgettes (Longest

Vegetable at **Knobbly Bottom** Fair three years running) had GONE.

"There were small soggy chunks all over the garden like someone had scoffed them in a hurry," said Fred.

"Who would scoff loads of disgusting courgettes?" I asked.

"Granddad says it was probably slugs, BUT I found this!" Fred replied, holding up the sandwich bag. "If you look closely, there is what appears to be a bite mark on the end of the specimen."

"And slugs do NOT leave bite marks," I finished.

"And this is not all. Come with me!" Fred said, and I followed him out of the shed and down the garden path to Mr Tibble's greenhouse, which is usually packed full of juicy red tomatoes. But you've probably already *guessed* that every single one of those tomatoes had been gobbled up. All that was left was juice and pips splattered across the glass of the greenhouse.

It was so GROSS we headed straight back to the shed for another EMERGENCY JAFFA CAKE.

"Granddad said that loads of other villagers have had the same thing happen to their vegetable patches. AND the local allotments have been hit!" said Fred. "It's the talk of the Knobbly Bottom gardening club!"

We BOTH agreed something way stranger than slimy bugs or hungry rodents was going on in **Knobbly Bottom**.

"But whoever or whatever is taking the food must be as sneaky as a snake in sunglasses," I said, "because they manage to eat everything really quickly without being spotted."

"Maybe they're invisible!" said Fred.

"Or hungry ghosts who have missed breakfast?" I said, a shiver creeping up my spine...

Then, just as I thought my spine couldn't get any more shivery, we heard a strange munching sound coming from behind some of the big boxes in the shed.

Fred looked at me, wide-eyed in terror. Could the greedy ghosts be in here with us right now? And were we next on the menu?

CHAPTER FOUR

A sneaky little scofferoo...

Munch, crunch, munch, crunch...

The munching sound behind the boxes was getting louder and louder.

MUNCH, CRUNCH, MUNCH, CRUNCH...

Fred quickly pulled a spatula from his belt, and I nodded towards the shed door. We needed to get out of there! We slowly, slowly backed away... Then a loud and horrifying sound broke the silence!

"BUUUUUUUURP..."

A huge but very human-sounding burp echoed through the shed, and then an empty Jaffa cake packet came flying over the top of the boxes...

"Got any more?" shouted Lily, her

chocolate-smeared face appearing from behind a particularly big crate.

That's the problem with little sisters. You can't trust them with emergency snacks.

She must have snuck into the **Beast Hunter Headquarters** while we were in Mr Tibble's greenhouse!

"Lily, you big scofferoo! Those were our emergency Jaffa cakes!" I yelled. "And this is a *secret* meeting!"

She smiled, wiping the crumbs from her face with her cape. "What's the secret meeting about?"

"I can't tell you because that is the whole point of a secret meeting!" I said. "And anyway, it's far too scary for you!"

"Super-Lily is not scared of hungry ghosts!" she said.

"Do you know that ghosts can't pick up cups? I'm NOT scared of anything that can't even pick up a cup."

She must have heard everything we said!

"Here, greedy ghosty-ghosty!" Lily called, before racing around the room excitedly. "Where are yooooooooou?"

Then Fred held his spatula up in the air and cleared his throat. "Right. All those in favour of investigating the Mystery of the Missing Food put your hand, or spatula, in the middle!" he said.

I put my hand in. It was followed by Fred's spatula, and then Lily put both hands in and cheered.

"Then let our second beast-hunting mission begin!" I said.

CHAPTER FIVE

The "stay-awake-out"

If we had learnt *anything* from the attack of the **vampire sheep** it was this: don't even *try* to tell grown-ups about evil beasts on the loose before you have actual PROOF to show them, because they will just tell you off for scaring your little sister and might even ban you from biscuits. That, and always keep some garlic bread in the freezer.

Fred said we should have a "stake-out" in his garden that night. This is apparently nothing to do with eating steaks but army code for **Sit And Watch Stuff In Case Anything Suspicious Happens.**

STAKE-OUT PLAN OF ACTION

1. Ask my mum if I can camp out in Fred's garden because he has a proper army camping tent.

2. When Mum says no (which she will because of her Saying No To Stuff hobby), ask her at least three times a minute and tell her I like her top (mums love that), and she will change her mind.

3. Make a scrumptious feast (1 x Fred's Irresistible Homemade Hamburger, 3 x bags of crisps, 4 x biscuits, half a jar of Nutella and leftover chicken dippers).

4. Accidentally make the feast so scrumptious that me and Fred eat most of it after dinner.

5. Make another scrumptious feast.

6. Leave scrumptious feast in a basket labelled SCRUMPTIOUS

FEAST at the end of the garden.

7.   Sit in tent with Fred's camera, torch, binoculars and four spatulas.

8.   Begin Stake-Out.

But the thing about stake-outs is this: they are soooooo boring. Especially when nothing suspicious is actually happening so you are basically just staring at a basket in the dark. And double especially when you have eaten your entire midnight feast by eight o'clock. They really need to rename them "stay-awake-outs" because by ten o'clock our eyes were so bored they were trying to close themselves. By ten thirty our mouths got so bored they started yawning for something to do. By eleven o'clock our bodies must have been bored too because they decided to make us fall asleep!

AND we accidentally stayed asleep until we were woken up by **FOOTSTEPS** outside our tent!

"There's something outside!" I whispered to Fred and looked at my watch. It was six o'clock in the morning!

Clomp, clomp, clomp.

"What is it?" hissed Fred.

Clomp, clomp, clomp. The footsteps seemed to be coming closer…

A shadow loomed outside the tent. It was human-sized but seemed to have an elephant's trunk! What on earth could it *be*? Another **Knobbly Bottom** beast? Me and Fred grabbed our spatulas.

The shadow leant over and then, slowly, steadily undid the zip on the tent.

I opened my mouth to scream…

"Cuppa tea, me dears?" It was just Mr Tibble
holding a massive teapot and two mugs on a
tray! It was a spout, not a trunk. PHEW.

"I thought you might want a nice hot drink!"
he said, placing the pot and tray on the ground.
"I would have brought you some brekkie, but I
expect you're both full to the brim after eating
that big basket of scrumptious food!"

Then he shuffled off back to the house, and Fred and I looked at each other in SHOCK.

We hadn't eaten that basket of food.

Which meant that while we were sleeping, someone – or *something* else – HAD.

CHAPTER SIX

A big fat smelly CLUE

"NO WAY! You will NOT believe this!" yelled Fred, who was peering inside the basket.

"What is it?" I asked, running over to join him at the scene of the crime.

Fred looked SO horrified that I wasn't sure I wanted to see what was inside. Was it a slimy giant slug? A family of demon mice? An evil pigeon?

I crept over to the basket and slowly peeped inside to find … **NOTHING** except leftover food, crumbs and empty packets.

"There's nothing there!" I said, relieved.

"Look again, Maggie!"

"It's just a leftover burger and wrappers, Fred!"

"Exactly! A *leftover* burger, Maggie! So they'll

eat your mum's soggy tuna sandwiches *and* my granddad's disgusting courgettes, but they won't touch my delicious, lovingly prepared homemade burger?" said Fred.

"What kind of beasts are they?"

"Maybe they're allergic to meat?" I suggested to make Fred feel better. He gets very upset if people don't like his cooking – even evil beasts apparently!

"They ate the chicken dippers!" Fred groaned. "Perhaps they were too full up to eat anything else?"

"No matter how full you are, you can always manage a freshly baked sourdough bun delicately smeared with organic tomato ketchup and filled with a homemade burger!" Fred sighed sadly.

Then I told Fred the rotten food thieves didn't deserve his delicious burger anyway, and that seemed to cheer him up enough to help me look for clues.

We searched the area for pigeon feathers, mouse droppings, slug slime or anything that might help us work out who or what the food thief was.

It was only when we were about to give up and go for breakfast that we found the most disgusting clue ever!

"Fred, you have got to see this!" I said, spotting something big, brown and smelly behind the shed. "Does Jeffrey **poo** in the garden?"

"Jeffrey would never **poo** in the garden!" said Fred.

At this point, I should probably tell you that Jeffrey is not an estate agent or geography teacher like most Jeffreys, but Mr Tibble's small and very cute Yorkshire terrier.

"He always waits until Granddad takes him for his morning walk! Besides, he was inside the house all night," said Fred, taking a photograph of the mysterious plop with his big camera as evidence.

Then we ran inside to ask Mr Tibble to come and have a look.

"Well, it's far too big to be Jeffrey's, that's for sure," said Mr Tibble, leaning over the mysterious dollop and picking it up with a dog-**poo** bag. "Big old badger, perhaps? I wouldn't worry about it, me dears. There's lots of wildlife out here in the countryside that could have snuck in for a number two."

So then we went and showed my mum the **poo** photo on Fred's camera, but she just said, **"THAT'S DISGUSTING!"** and that she didn't know or care what animal it might be from, especially when she was eating her Weetabix.

That's the trouble with grown-ups. They don't know *anything* about **poo**. In fact, Lily was more helpful.

"Have you seen any animal **poo** like this before, Lily?" I said, showing her the photograph.

"No, but the **Poo Patrol** might have!" she said.

"What on earth is the **Poo Patrol**?" I asked.

Lily told us that a man called Snaffle Snoot from the parish council had knocked on the door last night. (The parish council are a group of people in the village in charge of benches, fetes – and **poo patrols**, apparently.)

"He talked to Mummy for AGES about **poo**," said Lily, handing us a flyer. "He wanted us to join his **poo** club."

JOIN THE POO PATROL!

Come and clean our **Knobbly Bottom!**
Due to a recent spate of dog muckery,
we are calling for villagers to help us
SCOOP THAT POOP.

Let's clear our walkways and
footpaths of this dirty dung!
Meet on the green Sunday 9 a.m. to 1 p.m.

Free poo bags for all!

"Yuck!" I said, handing it to Fred.

"That's WEIRD because my granddad says people in **Knobbly Bottom** always clean up after their dogs!" said Fred. "I wonder if all this extra **poo** isn't *actually* from dogs! Maybe it's from the food thief who left us that plop last night!"

"The man told Mummy they think it might be foxes because people have also had their yucky food bins raided," said Lily. "And foxes love food bins."

Then Fred had the GROSSEST IDEA EVER.

"WE should join the **Poo Patrol**!" he said. "That way we could search for a match for the **poo** clue we found in my garden! It might lead us to the food thief's lair!"

I supposed it was a good (but gross) idea that might just work. "OK," I agreed.

"I'm coming too!" said Lily, grabbing her tea-towel cape.

And that is how we all ended up on the **most disgusting mission** ever.

CHAPTER SEVEN

The most disgusting mission EVER

I know what you are thinking. *If I wanted to read about **poo**, I would have bought* The Rise of the Big Poos *and NOT* The Rise of the Zombie Pigs. *And come to think of it, there hasn't been ONE single zombie or pig in this book yet, so I want my money back right now.*

Well, the thing is, before I tell you about the **zombie pigs**, I have to tell you how we *discovered* the **zombie pigs**, because that is just how a story works. I do not make the rules. And, unfortunately, how we discovered the **zombie pigs** involves a big old lump of **poo**.

But actually, you should enjoy this while you can, because when I DO tell you about those

HORRIFYING HOGS, you'll be so scared you'll *beg* me to talk about **poo** again.

I suppose I should get on with it or I'll never get to the creepy stuff.

My mum is super squeamish. That's not her superhero name, by the way. It means that whenever she sees anything disgusting she feels sick. Like, once we had to get off a bus two stops early because a boy next to us was picking his nose and eating it.

Anyway, this is why my mum wasn't very happy when I asked her if we could go on the

Poo Patrol later that morning. In fact, she looked even less happy than she does when she has to take me and Lily to a party at the soft-play centre.

BUT as soon as I had told her it might be a good way to "make friends" AND "get some fresh air" (she LOVES fresh air and friends), she said she would take us.

So later that morning, we met Snaffle Snoot on the village green. Snaffle is the head of the parish council, a pig farmer, AND you'll never guess whose dad he is? Yep! That bun grabber Celery Snoot!

You probably won't be surprised to hear that hardly anyone turned up to **Poo Patrol**. Apart from Snaffle, there was only me, Fred, Lily, my mum, Mr Tibble and Jeffrey. Even snooty Celery wasn't there.

"Friends, Knobbly Bottomers, Countrymen, lend me your ears!" announced Snaffle Snoot in the poshest voice I had ever heard. He was short and round with a huge head of curly red hair. He wore a fluorescent yellow overall saying **"Poo Patrol Leader"** in big letters, with green shorts and red wellies. "We shall scoop them from the footpaths. We shall scoop them from the bridleways. We shall scoop them from the hills and fields. We shall never surrender! With your help, the village *shall* be **poo**-free in time for tea."

Then he saluted, handed everyone some **poo** bags and marched us off towards the footpath on the other side of the green.

Fred pulled out the photo of the food thief's **poo** he had printed from his granddad's computer, and we began to scan the path for any matching muck. First we found NOTHING. But when we climbed over the stile into the **Knobbly Bottom** orchard, our muck luck changed!

"Over here," I called to Lily and Fred, who were using sticks to poke around in a ditch.

I pointed at a BIG lump of **poo** a few metres into the orchard. Fred ran over and pulled out his photo.

"They're the same shape and size, and I would remember that stink anywhere!" he said. "Which means the owner of the bum that left this in my garden must be nearby."

But when we glanced around the orchard, all we could see were apple trees, more apple trees and apples that had fallen off the apple trees!

"I trust you are going to bag that up, comrades!" said a familiar voice. Snaffle Snoot appeared behind us and examined the sloppy dung on the grass. "That's a two-bagger, I'd say. Leave it to me."

Then he put a **poo** bag on each hand and scooped up that giant **poop** as quick as lightning, like some kind of **poo**-scooping expert! That's when I had an idea.

"Mr Snoot," I asked in my most polite asking-about-**poo** voice. "What kind of animal do you think did that **poo**? It looks too big to be from a dog."

"Ah, now that's a tricky question ... for most

people! But luckily I am somewhat of an expert.
Or should I say – an ex**POO**t!"

He opened the bag and had a quick sniff.

"A pig!" he said, taking another sniff. "A three-year-old Saddleback, to be precise, and a lovely plump one at that! Must have wandered out of my farm. I'll have a word with Celery – she is tending to the little oinks at the moment. Anyway, go forth and scoop those **poops**, patrollers!"

As Snaffle stomped off out of the orchard, we peered past the apple trees and could just about make out some pigs in the field beyond. Maybe the missing food wasn't anything to do with the bad magic, after all? Could there just be some very normal but very greedy pigs wandering about **Knobbly Bottom**, eating and **poo**ing?

We decided we should go and take a quick look at the pigs JUST IN CASE. After all, we lived in **Knobbly Bottom**, not *Normally* Bottom.

And it's lucky we did, because over at Snoots' Farm something SUPER strange was happening...

CHAPTER EIGHT

A massive plate of biscuits to get the taste of poo out of your head

Sorry about all the **poo** in the last chapter. Here is a picture of a massive plate of biscuits to make up for it. You'll be glad to hear there is NO more **poo**, BUT things do get pretty scary, so enjoy these biscuits while you can.

CHAPTER NINE

The Famous Five had it SO easy

After deciding to investigate the pigs, me, Fred and Lily raced off across the orchard towards Snoots' Farm...

Well, we *would* have done if we had been lucky enough to be children from those olden-day books who are allowed to investigate burglars and baddies **ON THEIR OWN** all day long! In fact, sometimes their parents even packed ginger beer and sandwiches to take with them! What *actually* happened was this...

"MAGGIE AND LILY MCKAY, WHERE ON EARTH DO YOU THINK YOU'RE GOING?!" shouted my mum, rushing across the orchard after us.

And you might not be surprised to hear that she was NOT coming to give us some ginger beer but to tell us we weren't allowed to go running off on our own. Honestly, those Famous Five kids did not know how lucky they were. Then, when we told her we were only going to look at the pig farm, not WALK ACROSS FIRE, she said she would come with us (probably just to skive off **Poo Patrol**).

So we had NO choice but to let my mum walk across the orchard with us, while Mr Tibble and Snaffle Snoot continued **poo-patrolling** the main footpath.

As soon as Snaffle was out of sight, my mum sat under a shady apple tree and opened her coffee flask, while we ran towards the big gate that led to the farm.

But just before we reached it, I noticed something moving between the trees. Someone else was heading towards the pig farm!

I whispered to Fred and Lily to be quiet, grabbed their hands and ducked behind a bush. And that was when we saw…

Someone sneakily piling loads of juicy green apples into a wheelbarrow full of slops. *Someone* with two tight pigtails and a habit of stealing hot cross buns!

"It's Snaffle's daughter, Celery Snoot!" I whispered to Fred and Lily.

"What is she doing with all those apples?" asked Lily, as we watched Celery heave the wheelbarrow across the orchard and through the gate, towards a group of small pink pigs.

Fred took out his binoculars to have a closer look.

"Suspect appears to be feeding the pigs," he said, "A LOT of food. But everything seems normal."

Fred handed me the binoculars, and as the pigs tucked into their feast, I watched Celery push the now half-empty wheelbarrow into a huge pigsty at the other side of the field. It was shaped like a half circle and completely grey other than a few small windows and a big wide wooden door.

Meanwhile, the pigs in the field were munching away like very ordinary hungry animals, so it seemed as though there was nothing suspicious going on after all.

"Yep. Everything on Snoots' Farm looks normal to me!" I said, handing back the binoculars and secretly feeling a little disappointed there would be no more beast adventures this summer. "Just Celery and a bunch of boring pigs."

BUT as is usually the case in **Knobbly Bottom**, things did NOT stay normal for long. JUST as we were about to leave, something very odd happened...

"Are those pigs ... getting bigger?" Lily frowned.

Me and Fred looked back across the field. As the pigs munched merrily on Celery's slops, they appeared to GROW right before our eyes! Now, I know parents are always saying if you eat your greens you'll grow BIG and STRONG – but I don't think they mean in two seconds flat!

We got up from our hiding place and snuck over to the gate to get a closer look. "They're DEFINITELY growing!" I said.

And just when we thought things couldn't get any WEIRDER, the pigs started to turn as

GREEN as the apples they were eating... Then they grew UPWARDS and OUTWARDS until they had almost doubled in size. And the next thing we knew, their eyes were glowing bright green – and they began grunting angrily!

"Uh-oh!" I said to Fred. "What's happening to them?"

"It must be the bad magic!" he replied.

"We need to get closer," I said, pushing open the gate. "If we can take a photo as PROOF, we can show Gary, and he will get Nan Helsing to come home!"

"Good idea!" said Fred, taking the camera out of his rucksack. We told Lily to wait by the gate, and she didn't argue because the pigs looked pretty TERRIFYING, then we crept into the pig farm.

"They're so busy scoffing they probably won't even notice us!" I whispered, as we edged a little closer. "Quick! Take a picture while they aren't looking!"

But just as Fred held up his camera, the pigs gobbled the very last apple and looked *right at us* with hungry green eyes! They snorted noisily and began to trudge towards us, baring rotten brown teeth.

At this point we had no choice but to RUN FOR IT! As we raced back to the gate, we heard those greedy pigs chomping behind us, eating anything in their path! Weeds, twigs, mud and even...

"FRED!" I yelled, as he tripped over a log and tumbled to the ground, his camera going flying. The pigs' eyes glowed greedily, and they started shuffling faster… *I had to do something before they got their gross gobs on him!*

I turned back to help Fred, who was struggling to stand up in the slippery slop-covered grass.

"Shoo!" I shouted, but the pigs ignored me.

Then things went from BAD to WORSE as the largest one gave an extra-loud **OINK** and leant over Fred with its mouth wide open:…

Luckily, Fred whipped one of his emergency spatulas from his belt and waved it at the gruesome green pig! But you will NOT believe what that greedy gobbler did then! It grabbed that spatula right out of Fred's hands with its teeth and ATE IT!

Just then, there were two big *thuds*, and we looked up to see that two apples had landed on the ground a few metres from the scary swines!

"GET OFF FRED, YOU BIG GREEN MEANIES!" yelled Lily from the gate, holding up another big apple from the orchard.

Those evil oinksters must LOVE fruit because, thankfully, they forgot all about Fred and ran over to the juicy apples and started scoffing them instead!

"Nice work, Lily!" I yelled, helping Fred up. I suppose little sisters are quite useful sometimes.

"My camera!" cried Fred, pointing to where it lay between those horrid hogs.

"We'll have to leave it. Once they finish those apples they'll come after US!" I shouted, and we raced back across the field and into the orchard. We slammed the gate shut behind us in relief, just as the pigs started chomping on poor Fred's camera.

Now, I don't know a lot about pigs, but I was pretty sure they didn't *usually* eat cameras and spatulas.

"There is definitely something VERY wrong with those animals!" Fred said, as we watched the beasts plod across the field, chomping on everything in their path. "And there must be more of them hidden away inside that big pigsty – the ones who have been stealing all the food!"

"It's like they can't stop eating!" I said.
Fred nodded. "And that green, rotten-looking skin and creepy grunting... It's almost like they're..."

"ZOMBIE PIGS!" we said at the same time.

CHAPTER TEN

A very big pig problem

We *officially* had **zombie pigs** in **Knobbly Bottom** – SUPER-hungry ones who were sneaking out and eating everything they could get their trotters on.

So as soon as we had finished **Poo Patrolling** (sixteen plops successfully recovered according to Snaffle Snoot), me and Fred persuaded my mum and Mr Tibble to take us to the shop for a cold drink because **poop** scooping in a heatwave was thirsty work. Then, while my mum and Mr Tibble waited outside with Jeffrey and Lily, me and Fred raced inside to tell Gary EVERYTHING.

"Are you sure about this, skiddiwinks?" said Gary.

"YES! But we couldn't get PROOF because those mucky munchers ate Fred's camera!" I said, handing Gary three bottles of cold lemonade and some change my mum had given us. "'I'm sure they would have eaten him too given half a chance!"

"Well, I can't say I've heards of camera-eating **zombie pigs** before." Gary sighed. "But I'll double-check the gateway for bad magic leaks and try to get a message to Nan just in case."

"Should we warn the Snoots they have **zombie pigs** on their farm?" asked Fred.

"Hold your horseradishes until I've had a looksy into it – we can't go around telling folk about **Beastopia** willy nilly," groaned Gary.

He made us promise to NOT do anything until he had spoken to Nan, then told us to go before people saw *children* in the shop and ruined his reputation as a great and evil child-eater.

But Gary had said not to DO anything. He hadn't said not to FIND OUT anything. And with Nan away, we needed to learn everything we could about **zombie pigs**, including how to defeat them! So as soon as we got home, me and Fred went straight over to BHHQ to **Gather Intel**.

Now, if me and Fred were kids in a film, we would have spent DAYS and DAYS rooting around old libraries, reading dusty magic books and speaking to wise old men with beards, BUT luckily we are much cleverer than film kids so we just googled it.

MAGGIE AND FRED'S GOOGLE SEARCHES

How to defeat a zombie pig?

How to defeat a zombie?

Are zombies allergic to garlic?

Are pigs made from sausages?

What turns a pig into a zombie?

Who would win in a fight: a zombie pig or
a girl who had three karate lessons and
then got bored?

What is the opposite of a Jaffa cake?

What is best: an Oreo or a Jaffa cake?

The bad news is there was NOTHING about **zombie pigs**, but the good news is there was LOADS about actual normal **zombies** (and about biscuits – research is hungry work!). Anyway, here is what we found out about normal undead-type **zombies** like in the films.

ZOMBIE FACTS

1. They eat brains – not even with salt and pepper, just fresh from the head like total yucksters.

2. They are always **HUNGRY**, so can't stop eating.

3. All they do is walk around eating and grunting and moaning. **YUCK!**

4. The only way to defeat them is to destroy their brain! **DOUBLE YUCK!**
5. They do **NOT** exist in real life. Ha, well I have news for you, Google!

Annoyingly, none of this helped us. We couldn't go around destroying their brains because this would *also* destroy the poor innocent pig that had been "zombified"!

So we had NO choice but to wait for Nan Helsing to get back. She knew everything about every beast that ever lived!

Now I would LOVE to tell you that Gary managed to get in touch with Nan before those pesky pigs caused any more trouble, but I can't.

Because this is a book about BEASTS, and unfortunately beasts like nothing better than to cause a big fat load of trouble.

CHAPTER ELEVEN

Lily LITERALLY bites off
more than she can chew

The trouble started the very next morning on what turned out to be one of the **Worst Days Ever** because not one but TWO very bad things happened.

The first bad thing involved NOT eating any cake (again). And why didn't I get to eat any cake, you might ask? Well...

There was *supposed* to be a bake sale at the village hall to raise money for the church roof. One thing you should know about people in villages is that they love church roofs. They're always raising money to fix them. If you ask me, they should get God, aka the boss of churches, to make a new one. If he can create the whole world in a week, a church roof should only take a few seconds.

Anyway, everyone in the village had to bake something and take it along last night. (I think it was also OK if Tesco baked the cake and you just took it out of the packaging and put it in a plastic tub, because that is what my mum did.) Then they put them all on big tables so that the next morning you could go and buy them.

So my mum gave me and Lily a pound each to spend, and we hurried over to the village hall with Mr Tibble, Fred and Jeffrey. We were so excited we almost forgot about the **zombie pigs!** Even Beast Hunters in Training need a cake break sometimes.

BUT when we got there, we saw this sign on the door:

BOTTOM BAKE SALE CANCELLED

Unfortunately, today's bake sale is CANCELLED because every single bake TRAGICALLY disappeared last night. This means NO money shall be raised for the broken church roof on this occasion.

PUDDING PRICE

(Chairman of the Church Roof Committee and winner of the Great Bottom Bake Off)

* Coming soon! *
# BOTTOM'S GOT TALENT
Let's Raise (Money for) the Roof

KNOBBLY BOTTOM'S BIG CRACK
Comedy festival @ the village hall this winter!
All proceeds to the church roof

"The pigs!" I gasped as I stared open-mouthed at the sign.

"That's a bit rude, Maggie!" said my mum. "It's not the Church Roof Committee's fault the bakes disappeared!"

"I didn't mean that!" I said. "I mean, er … some greedy pigs must have eaten the cakes!"

"Pigs don't go around stealing cakes, Maggie!" said Mum. "I expect it was these mice that seem to be nibbling their way through the village!"

"My gardeners' club are saying it could be the work of rats!" said Mr Tibble, checking his buzzing phone. "It's the talk of the group. Noddy Lickers from Knobbers Way is calling it a ratastrophe!"

So we all stomped off home with NO cake, but luckily Fred asked if me and Lily would like to come and have some homemade apple pie in the BHHQ instead because he'd baked one for the bake sale last night but kept an extra one.

"Sixteenth rule of army training: always have a secret spare snack!" he said. "You never know when an enemy might snatch your supplies!"

A few minutes later we were in the BHHQ, about to start an **EMERGENCY ZOMBIE OUTBREAK MEETING** while we ate pie. The pigs were clearly getting even HUNGRIER if they had eaten a WHOLE bake sale. They needed to be stopped as soon as possible. Therefore, Mission Defeat the **Zombie Pigs** was back on. There was NO time to wait for Nan Helsing.

Fred put his big delicious-looking homemade apple pie on a crate and dashed back inside to get some ice cream to go with it, while I started writing ideas on the whiteboard.

"Any thoughts on how to defeat **zombie pigs**?" I asked Lily.

"*Mmm, chomp, umm, muuu,*" she answered.

"Why are you talking in that silly voice!" I said, turning to face her – and that's when I realized my little sister had taken a giant bite out of Fred's apple pie! "Lily, you're as greedy as the **zombie pigs**!"

As Fred came back in with the ice cream, I was just about to tell him that Lily was a big pie pincher when the second BAD thing of the day happened!

FIRST, Lily's cheeks seemed to swell up like a puffer fish…

THEN her tummy started to bulge…

NEXT her skin and eyes started to turn a little bit GREEN…

And then she started GROWING!

But before I could shout "MY LITTLE SISTER

IS TURNING INTO THE INCREDIBLE HULK!" Fred worked out what was happening.

"The apple pie!" he yelled, rushing over to Lily, whose mouth was still crammed with her big bite of pie. "I made it with apples from the **Knobbly Bottom** orchard! The same ones Celery fed to the pigs who turned into **ZOMBIES!**"

"The *apples* must have the bad magic in them!" I cried. "Spit it out, Lily! NOW!"

But Lily's face filled with panic, and the button popped off her shorts as her tummy grew even bigger! I realized I had NO choice but to prise open my little sister's mouth and scoop out that soggy piece of apple myself, while whacking her on the back (like I have seen people do on TV when there is a FOOD-STUCK-IN-MOUTH emergency).

Then, super slowly, THANK FLIPPING GOODNESS, poor Lily returned to her normal size and colour, and fell to the ground, coughing.

She looked very red-faced and confused, but she seemed OK.

"Are you all right, Lily?" I asked, wiping the sloppy green mess off my hand. Honestly, it was a good thing my Big Sister Bravery powers had kicked in to STOP me from thinking about how DISGUSTING it was.

"I'm so hungry," Lily replied, and then CAN YOU BELIEVE she only went to pick up another slice of apple pie? This is why little sisters should not be on missions to defeat **zombie pigs**! Luckily, Fred grabbed the plate and chucked the whole thing into one of his extra-large sandwich-evidence bags before she reached it.

I grabbed Lily by the shoulders. "Lily! That pie almost turned you into a zombie!" I shouted.

"Cool!" she said.

"Not cool at all!" I told her, shaking my head. "I can't believe how close I came to having a **GIANT ZOMBIE** for a sister."

"I just hope no one else in the village made pies from the orchard apples," Fred said shakily.

And that's when we realized we were facing a new, urgent mission. **Operation Get Rid of the Bad Magic Apples** – before we had a **zombie apocalypse** on our hands!

CHAPTER TWELVE

Beast hunters should NOT have to go shopping for shoes

The thing about getting rid of a massive orchard FULL of **zombie** apples is this: it is impossible. Especially when you only have three bin bags and NO ladder and quite small hands.

So we decided that the best thing to do was to tell Gary about the apples as soon as possible. As he is the actual Guardian of the Gateway to **Beastopia**, I bet he is fully trained in bad-apple destroying.

I took Lily home because she said she was starving (definitely a side effect from the bad apples as she had already eaten a whole tub of ice cream for the SHOCK). Me and Fred left her with a couple of biscuits while we went to the shop with Mr Tibble "to get more tea".

As soon as Mr Tibble went off to get the shopping, we told Gary EVERYTHING. Fred had even brought the soggy apple pie in a sandwich bag to show him.

Gary reached under the counter for what looked like a metal torch. He switched it on, and a bright white light shone on the apple pie. Then the strangest thing happened. When the light from the torch hit the pie, the whole slice glowed bright green!

"Oh, dear me!" gasped Gary, switching off the torch and staring in horror at the piece of pie. "Oh dear, oh dear. You're *right*. My bad-magic detector shows that the apples is riddled with the stuff!"

For someone who calls himself the **Great and Evil Child-Eater**, Gary suddenly looked quite scared.

"This is a case for a Helsing, all right," he mumbled. "She ain't replied to any of my messages yet, so I'll try ringing her at the hotel instead. Then I'll meets yous at the orchard to deal with these bad apples."

BUT when we went home to grab as many apple-picking bags as we could carry, my mum ruined EVERYTHING!

She said I *couldn't* go on an important mission with Fred because we were going on an important mission of our own this afternoon. But my mum is a big trickster because it wasn't an important mission at all – it was flipping SCHOOL SHOE SHOPPING, aka the most **boring** thing ever! So Fred had to go apple destroying without me.

Yep. That's right. My mum is STILL making me go to school in September. Even though I told her I am double super busy with beast hunting, she just said I have to go and "that's that". I don't see why I even need to go to school at all because I have Google and a calculator, and they know everything. Plus, they do NOT teach you the really important stuff.

IMPORTANT STUFF SCHOOL DOESN'T TEACH YOU

1. How to make a den out of sheets and pillows
2. How to make fire without any matches or lighters because your mum won't let you have them
3. How to save the world from EVIL BEASTS
4. Where all the hairbands go
5. How to make a catapult
6. How to do that cool whistle with two fingers
7. How to survive a zombie apocalypse
8. How to complete Super Mario
9. Kung-fu
10. How to fix a car (when our car broke down last summer my mum lifted the bonnet to have a look before admitting she had NO idea what she was looking for and then she said

they really should teach you these
things in school)

Also, I hate school shoes. They are too diggy-inny, but you're not allowed to wear trainers to school because FOR SOME REASON teachers don't like children having comfy feet when they're learning stuff. I bet I would know ALL my times tables by now if my feet were comfortable in the classroom.

BUT at least my mum said we could go for a milkshake AFTER we had bought our school shoes. That's the thing about mums. They NEVER let you do something FUN unless you do something BORING first. They're sneaky like that. Like when they make you eat one more spoonful of yucky vegetables before you can have dessert, or do your homework before you can watch cartoons. I am pretty sure this is BRIBERY and illegal, but obviously my mum thinks she is *above the law*.

She drove us to the nearest big town outside **Knobbly Bottom**, and after three hours of shopping I *still* couldn't find any school shoes. They were either too toey, too heely or too shoey. But luckily, just as my mum was saying we would have to go home with no milkshake, I suddenly remembered that the first pair of shoes I tried on probably did fit me, actually. I thought my mum would be pleased about this, but she was NOT! She just got all grumpy and marched us back to the shop.

And the good news is Lily *also* realized the first shoes she tried on fitted *her*, so we finally went to the café for posh milkshakes (chocolate orange for me, banana for Lily, weird yucky cold coffee with ice cubes in it for my mum)! Mum said as it was so hot we could sit at a table outside, so we did – and that was when I saw something SUPER suspicious…

There was a bakery opposite with loads of expensive-looking cakes and bread in the window, and guess who was coming out with SIX bags of cake... CELERY SNOOT!

"Why is Celery Snoot buying *six bags* of cake?" I asked Mum and Lily.

"What a greedy guts!" said Lily.

"Don't be rude, Lily!" said my mum. "She's probably having a party or something."

But that's when things got even weirder! When my mum went inside the café to pay, a big truck pulled up outside the bakery.

"Pop them in the boot, my little dumpling!" yelled a familiar posh voice out of the open window. It was Celery's dad, Snaffle Snoot.

Snaffle pressed a button and the huge boot popped open.

You'll never guess what was inside – MORE cakes! Big ones, small ones, cupcakes and Victoria sponges, all piled up on big trays. Celery and her dad must have bought everything from every bakery in town!

"OK, no more cakes now, my little pork pie,"

Snaffle shouted out of the truck window. "This is the third lot this week!"

"Just a few more, Daddy!" said Celery as two bakers came out carrying trays and trays of yet MORE cake!

Celery gestured for them to put the trays in the truck while Snaffle Snoot handed them a big wad of money.

"Are you sure the pigs will eat all these cakes, dumpling?" Snaffle asked his daughter. "It seems like an awful lot."

"Yes!" replied Celery. "They're growing piggies with big appetites, Daddy!"

"Of course, my cute casserole!" said Snaffle. "Why don't I pop down and see them later?"

"NO, DADDY!" snapped Celery. "I, er ... have them on a very strict routine to prepare for the Golden Grunt and they can't be disturbed. Do not come down to the pigsty!"

"As you wish," said Snaffle as Celery got into the truck and slammed the door behind her.

I turned to Lily, who looked as confused as me.

"Why would Celery feed her pigs all those cakes?" I said. "And what the heck is the Golden Grunt?"

One thing was for sure – Celery Snoot was definitely up to something. And I was going to find out what!

CHAPTER THIRTEEN

Please don't tell my mum about anything in this chapter or I will be in BIG trouble

When we got back from town, I wanted to go *straight* over to Fred's to tell him all about the INTEL I had gathered on Celery. PLUS, I needed to find out whether Gary had destroyed all the bad apples! But my mum said it was too late and we were going to have dinner and an early night.

At least the pigs had the cakes from Celery to keep them going, so they wouldn't need to go out gobbling bake sales and vegetable patches while we were in bed. Or so I thought...

It all started later that night when I was eating my secret stash of jelly babies in bed to get the thoughts of those hideous hogs out of my head before I went to sleep. Which is a very sensible thing to do if you ask me. BUT then my mum came in and got all cross at me for eating sweets in bed when she'd told me not to. (This was a LIE because she *actually* said no sweets *before* bed, not no sweets *in* bed.)

Anyway, she took my sweets away (probably so *she* could eat them), and I was lying there for ages trying to decide whether I would rather have a biscuit or cherry-flavoured hand. I had just decided biscuit (so I could dip it in tea) when I heard a WEIRD noise coming from our back garden!

It sounded like when you snap a big stick in half but a million times louder. Then, as if that wasn't strange enough, it was followed by a loud slip-slopping like when you suck the last of your milkshake up through a straw.

I climbed out of bed and peered between my bedroom curtains. It was really dark, but I could just about make out two four-legged figures by our shed! It was my duty as a

Sort Of Beast Hunter While Nan Helsing Was Away to investigate. The first thing I needed to do was get a closer look at the intruders, so I snuck downstairs to peep out of the kitchen window.

I slowly pulled open the curtains, only to get one of the BIGGEST shocks of my life – because I saw a GLOWING FACE peering back at me through the window…

A glowing face wearing a head torch and full combat gear, and holding a big wooden spoon. FRED!

He knocked gently on the window and waved at me with his spoon.

"Maggie! We have a CODE Z, I REPEAT CODE Z," he said, just loud enough for me to hear.

I opened the back door and glanced down the garden behind him, but the shadowy shed creatures had completely gone.

"What the heckedy-doo-dah is a Code Z?" I asked.

"**Zombie emergency!** I saw **zombie pigs** munching on our garden bench, so I came out to investigate!" he said. "It looks like they had a nibble on your shed too. When I saw you peek out of your bedroom window, I thought I'd better warn you."

I slipped on my nearest shoes (which happened to be my new school shoes) and a jacket.

"What are you doing, Maggie?" asked Fred.

"We HAVE to find out more about these pigs!" I replied, tiptoeing out of the back door. "I reckon their headquarters MUST be that massive pigsty at Snoots' Farm. Let's check it out NOW and see what they're up to!"

So me and Fred snuck out of the front gate on to the quiet street. All the houses were in darkness, and the only light came from an old-looking lamp post on the other side of the green. As we headed for the farm, Fred explained how Gary *still* hadn't been able to get hold of Nan, but he'd left an urgent message with her hotel. But he *had* borrowed Nan's tractor. Fred had helped him gather up all the bad apples, then Gary had burned them all on a bonfire.

"Gary even sprayed the tree roots with holy water so next year's apples will be totally normal," Fred said. "So at least no more pigs can turn into **zombies**. That means we might only be dealing with a few of them!"

"I reckon there must be MORE than a few!" I said, and I told Fred all about sneaky Celery and the cakes!

"Wow, I'm surprised they're still hungry after six bakery loads of cakes!" said Fred. "Do you really think she knows they're **zombies**?"

"I wouldn't put it past her." I replied. "She probably wants to make an army of **zombies** to help her do evil stuff like steal hot cross buns!"

"Classic baddy move!" said Fred. "Raise an army of muscly meatheads and make them do all your dirty work!"

"Hopefully we will find a few clues about what she's up to in the pigsty," I hissed as we crept across the dark, appleless orchard and through the gate into the Snoots' field.

The HUGE pigsty towered in the distance. The grey metal building glistened eerily in the moonlight as we slowly walked towards the door...

"It's the biggest pigsty I've ever seen!" said Fred.

"And the stinkiest!" I said, holding my nose as a rotten stench drifted out from under the door.

"Right, let's see if the coast is clear!" I said, opening the big wooden door a tiny bit and stepping inside. "NO pigs, but YUCKEDY-DOO-DAH!"

And that is when we saw why this place had such a revoltsome **STINK**.

Now before you say, *"No more **poo**, Maggie, you promised – we cannot take any more **poo**!"* I'm happy to tell you that while there was NO poo in the pigsty (that we could see), what we DID see was almost as disgusting.

The whole place looked like someone had taken fifty BINS and emptied them all over the floor. And I don't mean the recycling bin where you just put cardboard and stuff. Or even the one where you put rubbish you can't recycle, but the WORST bin of all: the FOOD BIN where my mum makes us put the leftovers! Apparently, the council turn it into compost for gardens, but why *anyone* would want to put old baked beans and sandwich crusts on their flower beds I do NOT know.

There were huge piles of chicken bones, fish heads, rotten apple cores and banana peel, and loads and loads of empty cupcake wrappers that were halfway up to the roof. There was other random rubbish scattered about too, as if they had raided a SKIP in their search for food – broken toys, old clothes, mouldy mattresses and cardboard boxes.

But then something happened that made the stinky stench seem like the least of our worries… Suddenly we heard heavy footsteps coming from *outside* the pigsty. Except these steps didn't sound like they were being made by actual FEET.

They sounded very much like they were being made by **TROTTERS**!

CHAPTER FOURTEEN

The pig princess and her army

Me and Fred dived behind a pile of empty cardboard boxes and held our breath as, one by one, the **zombie pigs** piled into the sty – looking bigger and scarier than ever.

The two biggest beasts yawned and stretched out on top of one of the mountains of YUCKNESS as if they were lounging on a luxury beach! One of them even lay on an old mattress and started chucking pieces of rotten food up into the air and catching them in its massive mouth. This is not easy to do when you have trotters instead of hands, so a lot of the gross grub landed on his head! Meanwhile, a swarm of smaller swine wandered around, aimlessly sniffing at the pongy piles of rubbish.

Suddenly the largest pig stood up on its hind legs – which made it look even *more* gigantic – and put its trotters on its hips.

Then just when you thought things couldn't get any weirder than PIGS who turn into **ZOMBIES**, well, this happened...

"Hey, you guuuuuuuys!" called the largest pig, smiling.

All the other pigs turned to look up at her.

"I don't know about you lot, but I'm STILL hungry," she announced. "And I'm dead fed up of scrounging around this village for scraps!"

The other pigs oinked and nodded in agreement.

"So I have a totes *oinksome* idea," she said, picking up a broken toy tiara and placing it on her head. "We will eat like NO pig has ever eaten before. We will FEAST like kings and queens! It will be EPIC. Who's with me? **Hogroll?**"

Then she picked up a banana skin and threw it at the shorter but fatter zombie pig who was lying lazily on the dirty old mattress, wearing a manky-looking red baseball cap.

"Too right I'm with ya, **Swinetta**!" he said, yawning before standing up on his hind legs. "We're gonna take over the world!"

"We're gonna do better than that, hun," said this scary "**Swinetta**", picking up an old baby's bib that was nestled among the rubbish and tossing it to **Hogroll**. "We're gonna EAT it!"

"EAT THE WORLD! Eat the world! Eat the world!" **Hogroll** chanted, tying the "I LOVE MUMMY" bib around his neck and licking his lips.

"Soon we'll never be hungry again!" said **Swinetta**, straightening her tiara as the entire swarm of pigs grunted in excitement.

"This is CODE Z times ten!" whispered Fred, turning to me with a look of horror on his face.

"Yep," I agreed, as chants of "EAT THE WORLD" echoed across the dark pigsty. "They're even more dangerous than we thought!"

"We need to get out of here before they spot us!" I said, pointing to a small window behind Fred. Luckily, all the pigs had their backs to us as they grunted adoringly at **Swinetta**, so we snuck over to the window and quietly pushed it open.

"Go!" I whispered to Fred, and he climbed out into the dark field. I was about to hitch myself up after him when some chilling words filled the air.

"OMG, it's humans!" yelled **Swinetta** – and I turned to see the pongy pig princess staring right at me, licking her lips. "Fresh ones. Anyone for a midnight feast?"

CHAPTER FIFTEEN

When zombie pigs get hangry!

"Get her!" squealed **Swinetta**, heading towards me as I scrambled through the window. "We can't have them telling everyone about us and our secret plans!"

But one good thing about **zombie pigs** is this: they have really BIG heads that can easily get stuck in windows – which is exactly what happened to **Swinetta** when she tried to clamber out after me!

So while her partner in grime, **Hogroll**, tried to pull her free, me and Fred managed to make our escape.

We RACED across the dark field as fast as we could, but the smaller pigs trotted out of the pigsty and followed us! Although they weren't very fast because their never-ending hunger meant they stopped to nibble at anything they came across: grass, mud and even a big cow pat!

Luckily, we soon lost them in the darkness and stole back through the orchard, along the green and back to our houses.

"We'll go to Gary first thing in the morning and tell him we need Nan Helsing to come home NOW!" I said, and Fred agreed.

"This is a beast emergency!"

The **zombie pigs** were bigger, badder and even **HUNGRIER** than ever!

I managed to get into bed without waking up my mum or Lily, and I was sooooo tired I fell asleep as soon as my head hit the pillow.

BUT can you believe that VERY early the next morning I was *rudely* woken up by my mum waving muddy shoes in front of my face!

"Why on earth have you been in the mud in your NEW school shoes, Maggie?" demanded my mum.

"So I wouldn't get my socks dirty," I replied. "Lucky I put them on, really."

But for some reason my mum didn't think it was lucky. She got cross and banned ME from watching cartoons, which was so unfair! I told her that if the silly old shoes couldn't stop socks from getting dirty without getting ruined, then that was THEIR fault, NOT mine. After all, it was their ONE job. So they should be the ones banned from cartoons, NOT me.

Then I told her I had much more important things to worry about than cartoons today anyway. But my mum said the only important thing I had to worry about was cleaning my shoes. UGH! I would just have to clean them super quickly and then find Gary!

So after breakfast, Lily was "helping" me clean my shoes in the garden (basically just squirting them with her water pistol), when Fred climbed over the fence, waving a piece of paper.

"Guess what!" he said. "My granddad is on the parish council, and this morning he was called to an emergency meeting. Something really BAD happened last night!"

"Worse than almost getting eaten by a swarm of **zombie pigs**?" I asked.

Fred sighed. "Not quite, but it seems we didn't just make the pigs angry. We made them HANGRY. Listen to this!"

KNOBBLY BOTTOM PARISH COUNCIL EMERGENCY MEETING

Re: Night of Doom

Summary of events:

1. All vegetables devoured from Knobbly Bottom allotments.
2. Village shop stockroom broken into, and all foodstuffs stolen

other than a family-sized bottle of tomato ketchup.

3. All blackberries on the bushes on Knobs Hill have disappeared.

4. Snaffle Snoot's garage broken into and barbecue fridge raided. Six burgers, ten buns, lettuce and all condiments missing except half a bottle of tomato ketchup.

5. Seventeen wheelie bins tipped over and raided.

6. Village sign nibbled.

7. Every flower bed in the village has been chewed on!

"Granddad says the council have now decided it *can't* be rats or mice!" said Fred, after he had finished reading us the list. "They think it must be something bigger!"

"Dinosaurs?" asked Lily.

"Not quite that big…" said Fred.

"Baby dinosaurs!" yelled Lily.

"No. They're blaming foxes!" replied Fred.

"Ha! This is definitely the work of the **zombie pigs**!" I said. "They must have gone on a *hangry* rampage after we escaped last night."

"What are we going to do?" said Fred. "They seem to eat anything!"

"Apart from tomato ketchup," said Lily. "Which is weird because tomato ketchup is the BEST."

"Lily's right!" I said, peering at the list. "Look. They didn't eat the tomato ketchup from Gary's stockroom OR Snaffle's barbecue fridge!"

Fred's eyes lit up. "And remember they didn't touch my homemade burger? It must've been because of the ketchup! Not because there was anything wrong with my cooking!"

I stared at Fred. "Maybe ketchup is to **zombie pigs** what garlic is to vampires! They must be allergic to it. This must be how we defeat them!"

Fred looked worried. "But we need to wait until Nan gets back!" he said.

"Fred, they're planning to eat the world and everything in it – which might even include all of us! And we still haven't managed to get hold of Nan. We need to stop them NOW! What if … we just bake them some special cakes?" I said because I knew Fred would *not* be able to resist the chance to bake. "They must have a sweet tooth. Remember how many Celery bought them?"

"What sort of special cakes?" asked Fred, clearly already excited about the idea of baking.

"Tomato ketchup cakes!" I said.

"YUCK!" said Fred.

"YUM!" said Lily, who loves cakes *and* ketchup.

"Nan will be SO pleased when we manage to banish the beasts without her!" I said.

"OK," said Fred. "First, we update Gary on *everything* we know. Then we BAKE!"

And this is how we came up with an AMAZING PLAN that would ~~maybe hopefully~~ definitely STOP those greedy **zombie pigs** before they ate the world and everything – and everyone – in it.

But the thing about amazing plans to defeat **zombie pigs** is this: they can be very, very dangerous.

CHAPTER SIXTEEN

The great beastly bake-off

As soon as I had cleaned my shoes, my mum agreed to take us to the shop for ingredients to bake cakes at Fred's house.

"Why on earth do you need all that ketchup?" she asked, spotting six bottles in Fred's basket.

"Well, actually, in the army they bake with tomato ketchup instead of sugar because sugar is really hard to get in war zones," I said, thinking quickly. "Isn't that right, Fred?"

"Er … yes," stuttered Fred.

"Really?" said my mum. "I would have thought in a war zone it would be harder to get hold of tomato ketchup."

"Don't be silly, Mum. Everyone knows armies always have loads of tomato ketchup," I said.

"They don't leave home without it, right, Fred?"

Fred nodded. "Mmm."

"Well, I must 'ketchup' on my army knowledge!" My mum laughed as if she'd told the funniest joke ever.

Then my mum said she would wait outside in the sunshine (parent-speak for look at her phone for a bit).

Fred put three dozen eggs, heaps of butter, three bags of flour and loads of ketchup on the counter, then we told Gary all about the **zombie pigs**' plan to EAT THE WORLD, and about that suspicious, cake-buying sneaker Celery who might be in on it!

Gary looked unusually flustered. "I am no beast expert like Nan. I just keep the gateway safe, me. I've left her a squillion messages. As soon as Nan calls me back, I'll ask her what to do. We do NOT want to cause panic! Whatever happens, we MUST keep the secret of **Beastopia**."

"Don't worry, Gary – we have a plan!" I said.

"No plans, skiddiwinks. These beasts are too dangerous," said Gary firmly, scanning Fred's shopping. "Just promise me you will stay away from 'em till Nan gets back."

"But what if we just—" I started.

"No." Gary shook his head firmly.

Me and Fred shared a look. The thing about genius plans to defeat **zombie pigs** with tomato ketchup is this: if you tell a grown-up, they might not let you carry them out. AND, even worse, they might refuse to sell you the ingredients. So we kept our mouths shut and nodded.

We were almost certainly RIGHT about the tomato ketchup, so it HAD to be worth a try. Especially as it just happened to be National Cake Giveaway Day!

WOULD YOU LIKE ONE THOUSAND CAKES?

To celebrate National Cake Giveaway Day, we are giving away one thousand delicious cakes for FREE!

Simply come to the back door at 9 The Green at 7 p.m. and claim your goodies.

See you there, cake fans!

Now, before you tell everyone you know to give you a cake right NOW because it is National Cake Giveaway Day, then I am sorry to tell you that I just made it up. It is not an actual day at all. That is how clever this plan is.

And it got even *more* clever because we would ONLY tell Celery about the cake giveaway! There was no way she would be able to resist the chance to get some more sweet treats for her hungry hogs, especially after her dad said he wouldn't buy her any more.

So **Operation Ketchup Cakes** was ON!

First, Fred went and stuck the cake giveaway sign on the gate of the Snoots' pig field while walking Jeffrey with Mr Tibble. And guess what he saw! Celery, dragging her wheelbarrow towards the sty – but all she had in it was a bag of frozen peas, a tin of mackerel and three potatoes. She must have been running out of food! Which meant she would definitely NOT be able to resist our giveaway.

The next thing we had to do was BAKE. I told my mum I was going to Fred's, and Fred told his granddad he was at mine, when really we were both in Fred's kitchen baking one thousand ketchup cakes while Mr Tibble was at choir practice.

But the problem with baking one thousand cakes while your friend's granddad is at choir

practice is this: you probably won't have enough EGGS or TIME to actually bake them all. In the end we only had eighty-nine, but that would just have to do.

Then all we had to do was WAIT for Celery to come calling!

Just when we were starting to think she

hadn't seen the sign, we heard a stomping sound coming from Fred's back garden.

Clomp, stomp, clomp...

"Celery?" whispered Fred, walking towards the back door.

Clomp, stomp, clomp... Clomp, stomp, clomp...

The noise got louder. It sounded like more than one person!

CLOMP, STOMP, CLOMP...

"Open up, babes! We're here for one thousand cakes!" came a familiar snorty voice from the other side of the door.

That was not Celery.

That was **Swinetta!**

CHAPTER SEVENTEEN

The "sauce" of the problem

"We saw the sign and we've come for CAKE!" yelled another greedy voice from Fred's garden.

Hogroll was here too!

Then I peeped through the kitchen window and saw that it wasn't just **Swinetta** and **Hogroll** knocking at the door – there were about SIX other **zombie pigs** all standing in Fred's back garden looking very, very hungry!

"Oh no!" I whispered to Fred as the pigs spotted me at the window. "They must be able to READ! Celery didn't see our sign – *they* did!"

"Little kids, little kids, let us come in!" said **Swinetta**, knocking loudly on the door with her huge trotter. **"Or we'll BITE your HOUSE DOWN!"**

"Where's these free cakes?" snorted **Hogroll**, munching his way through a plant pot he had picked up off the patio before spitting it out in disgust.

"Let us in by the hairs on our *gorgeous* chins!" said **Swinetta**, her face appearing in the window. "I heard it was National Cake Giveaway Day so you **HAVE** to give us cakes."

"Open. This. Door!" added **Hogroll**.

"What do we do?" panicked Fred. "They'll wreck the place!"

Then there was a huge bang as **Hogroll** SLAMMED himself against the door, knocking it wide open!

Luckily, because I am a hide-and-seek champion, it only took me a split second to find a brilliant hiding place. Me and Fred managed to dive under the kitchen table, just as **Swinetta**, **Hogroll** and the smaller **zombie pigs** barged into the house.

Suddenly the kitchen was TOTAL chaos. But the good news was that the pigs had forgotten all about *us* as they hungrily gobbled up all the freshly baked cakes on the sideboard. From under the table, we could see loads of soggy crumbs and pig slobber falling to the floor. **Zombie pigs** were even messier eaters than Lily!

Now, I would love to tell you that once the beastly baddies had finished the tomato-ketchup

cakes, they immediately turned back into normal pigs, then went back to their farm for a lovely big nap and we all lived happily ever after.

But unfortunately that did not happen.

The horrible hogs DID finish all the cakes, but they did NOT turn back into ordinary pigs! In fact, they got **BIGGER** and **HUNGRIER** with each bite!

Then, just as I was about to tell Fred about a Plan B I had just come up with called "RUN FOR YOUR FLIPPING LIFE", there was a low groaning sound. This was followed by another groan, a moan, and then more groans... *Was the ketchup working after all?*

We peeped out and saw the **zombie pigs** rubbing their enormous tummies. They reminded me a bit of Lily when she accidentally ate THREE margaritas at Pizza Hut because she thought my mum had said it was an Eat All Of It Buffet, not an All You Can Eat Buffet. Anyway, me and Fred smiled at each other, thinking this was the bit where they transformed back into normal pigs and we SAVED THE DAY.

But then **Swinetta** opened her mouth ... and did the loudest burp EVER.

The next thing we knew, all the pigs started burping – **AND NOT JUST FROM THEIR MOUTHS BUT FROM THEIR BUMS!**

Soon the entire kitchen was full of smelly zombie burp and trump fumes. It was the most *disgusting* thing I had ever seen (and smelt)! Even more disgusting than the time Michael Cameron from my old school threw up on baby Jesus in the Nativity play. (This was especially GROSS because I was Mary, aka the person HOLDING the baby! Anyway, he panicked and shouted "AMEN" before being sick all over a wise man. Worst nativity ever. Or "NaVOMITy" as my mum called it.)

And the *worst* thing was that those bum-belching beasts were showing NO signs of turning back into ordinary pigs!

"At least we know why they don't eat tomato ketchup," whispered Fred, as an extra-loud piggy pump echoed across the kitchen. "It gives them tummy ache!"

"Still hungry!" belched **Hogroll**, and we heard Mr Tibble's kitchen cupboards creaking open and closed. Can you believe they wanted MORE FOOD?

I glanced out from under the table to see **Hogroll** and **Swinetta** emptying the contents of the fridge into their huge mouths.

"We need to stop them before they *literally* eat me and Granddad out of house and home!" whispered Fred. "But how?"

Then I had an idea!

"Fred, the internet said that to defeat a normal zombie you have to destroy its brain, right?"

"Yes, but we don't want to hurt the pigs, remember?" replied Fred, looking horrified.

"I know, but what if instead of *destroying* their

brains, we just give them brain-ache?" I said.
"Brains MUST be their weak spot, so if we can give them a headache it might slow them down enough for us to escape."

"That could work," said Fred. "But how do you give a pig a headache?"

I suggested we use **BOOKS** because my mum always gets a headache the day after she has been to book club. Sometimes it is soooo bad she has to stay in her pyjamas ALL morning, drinking water.

"That might work, but funnily enough there are no books UNDER THE KITCHEN TABLE." Fred started to panic as a half-eaten wooden spoon fell to the floor. "Wait, I've got it!" He suddenly shouted, "Alexa, play heavy metal really loudly!"

As you have probably guessed, Alexa isn't a girl who lives in Fred's kitchen but one of those speakers that plays music when you ask it to. You don't even have to say "please".

Right away, a loud, screechy, shouty sort of music started BOOMING through the kitchen. The singer seemed to be very angry about something. The music was so BAD I had to put my hands over my ears to stop it giving ME a headache!

"Fred! Well done!" I shouted over the music, as we peeked out from under the table to see all the **zombie pigs** with their trotters over their ears, groaning.

"OH MY DAYS! What the trot is that noise?" yelled **Swinetta**, heading for the door. "It's whack! Let's get out of here."

"It's working! They're going!" I shouted.

"Granddad once told me that the music my dad listened to when he was a teenager used to give him a headache. And it was something called 'heavy metal'," said Fred, looking pleased with himself.

BUT unfortunately he didn't look pleased for long, because just when we thought it was safe

to come out of our hiding place, the headachey metal music STOPPED.

This was super weird because Fred hadn't said "ALEXA, STOP MUSIC!" So either Alexa was broken OR ... someone or *something* had pulled out the plug.

Then a shadow crossed the kitchen, and we saw two big fluffy feet walking towards the table...

CHAPTER EIGHTEEN

You might not be surprised to hear we were in BIG trouble

"What on EARTH has happened in here?" shouted a very familiar voice. "Mr Tibble? Fred, Maggie!"

Fred and I slowly crawled out from under the table and came face to face with my mum, who was looking the angriest I had ever seen anyone look while wearing big fluffy slippers. She must have heard the music and come to investigate!

"WHAT ON EARTH HAVE YOU BEEN DOING?" she yelled, and we looked around at Mr Tibble's kitchen. Cake crumbs and empty food wrappers were everywhere. The fridge had been ransacked, and empty tins and half-eaten packets of food had been chucked across the floor. Flour and tomato ketchup were smeared all over the cupboards and walls. It was a *mess*.

"Er, baking?" I replied.

You probably won't be surprised to hear that at this point in the story, me and Fred were in very BIG trouble. Even though I told my mum that Celery's pigs had made all the mess, NOT us, she still told me off and said pigs do not break into houses and eat eighty-nine cakes.

When Mr Tibble came back from choir practice a few minutes later, he thought the house had been burgled before my mum explained. Then even after HOURS of cleaning up and saying sorry to Mr Tibble, my mum still said she was "very disappointed" and grounded me for a week!

I was sooooo TIRED from all the baking, hiding and cleaning that I did NOT have the energy to argue. But the next morning I had plenty to say about the whole thing!

"What if there is a fire or a flood or a massive spider on the loose?" I said. "Do I STILL have to stay in the house?"

Mum told me not to be silly because obviously I could leave the house if there was an emergency!

"But there IS an emergency!" I said. "I need to save the world from the **zombie pigs** that wrecked Mr Tibble's kitchen last night!"

"Oh, really?" said my mum. "An emergency like when you told me a gang of cheeky squirrels snuck in through your window and messed up your bedroom?"

"NO!" I said.

"Or when you said the neighbour's kitten had broken into our house and got green paint all up the kitchen walls?"

"Well…"

"They were human handprints, Maggie, and cats do not have hands!" snapped my mum.

"But the **zombie pigs** are real, and EVERYONE is in danger!" I cried.

"In that case, all the more reason for you to stay safely in the house!" said my mum, thinking she was SO clever.

Anyway, being grounded wasn't actually that bad because me and Lily spent all morning making up an EPIC show called *Wonderwoman and Super Mario the Musical* with sixteen songs and twelve costume changes. But GUESS WHAT! When we asked my mum to come and watch the sequel (*Wonderwoman and Super Mario: the Rap Battle*) she suddenly decided that I was ungrounded and could go and play in the garden.

But obviously I had far more important things to do – I still had a **zombie aPIGalypse** to stop! Me and Lily headed straight for the BHHQ to find Fred.

"Knock-a-doodle-doo!" I shouted Fred's latest password at the door, but there was no answer.

I knew Fred was inside because I could hear him talking to someone!

I have not even been grounded for a whole day yet – surely he hasn't got a new beast hunting gang already? I thought.

"Knock-a-doodle-doo, open this door, Fred!" I shouted again.

"Who is it?" came Fred's voice from the other side of the door.

"Fred, you know jolly flipping well it's me and Lily; we're the only ones who know the password!" I said.

"FRED TIBBLE, DO YOU READ ME? OVER," said another voice from inside the shed.

"Fred!" I shouted. "Who is that?"

Finally, the door creaked open, and a very excited-looking Fred let us in. He ran over to a laptop that was sitting on a crate and pressed some of the keys.

"What are you doing playing computer games when we have **zombie pigs** to deal with?" I asked as me and Lily sat on two big beanbags and opened up our BHHQ secret sweet stash. "And who were you talking to?"

"Nan Helsing!" Fred grinned. "I was able to contact her using some powerful magic."

"Oh, cool!" I said, and I got all excited about seeing some real magic right here in the shed, but then Fred pointed to the computer.

"YOU'VE GOT IT ON MUTE, NAN!"
Fred called to the dark, flickering shadow on
the screen.

"Ah, you're on a video call!" I said.

This is NOT magic. My mum does loads of
them for work and they sound very boring. All
they do is shout "Can you see me, John?" and

"Your microphone's off, Pamela!" to each other.

"Step back, Nan! All I can see is forehead!" said Fred. "And you need to UNMUTE!"

"HELLOOOOOOOO!" The flickering shadow slowly turned into a confused-looking Nan Helsing in enormous purple sunglasses. "Am I zoomering now, OVER?"

"We can hear you, Nan, but you're breaking up a bit," said Fred, as Nan stepped back, revealing a luxurious swimming pool in the background. "And you don't need to say 'over'."

"Right, I gotta be quickedy-splits because it's water polo in five minutes. Over!" she said, popping on a massive beach hat. "Gary rang me in a right old state, so I said I'd get in touch before you got yourselves into trouble. What's this about a little zombie pig problem?"

"Er, two HUGE problems called **Swinetta** and **Hogroll**, actually! And they have a whole gang of slightly smaller swine that do anything they say. How do we stop them?"

"We tried feeding them tomato-ketchup cakes, but it just gave them a bad tummy!" said Fred.

"Cakes?" Nan laughed. "You gave **zombie pigs** cakes? Oh dear, oh dear, oh dear. You don't want to be feeding them greedsters anything at all. Every time a zombie pig eats, it GROWS!"

I shot a worried look to Fred. The pigs were eating **NON-STOP**! No wonder they were massive!

"Celery Snoot is feeding them so much food," said Fred. "We wonder if she might be in on it."

"Those Snoots are crafty old boots, but I can't see them turning their precious pigs into terrifying beasts of doom," said Nan. "They know nothing about Knobbly Bottom's bad magic. The good news is, if she is keeping them well fed with cakes and whatnot, they won't want to cause her any harm."

I looked at Fred. Nan was usually right, but I was still SURE that sneaky Celery was up to something.

"I'm getting the next flight home, so I'll sort this whole messeroo out when I get back! Keep this to yourselves, lock all your doors and windows, and do not go wandering around at night," said Nan. "Those swine could swallow you kiddies up like a sea lion snacking on a sardine. Over."

"But HOW will you stop them, Nan?" I asked. "They're getting bigger by the day!"

"The only way to defeat a zombie pig is not to feed 'em anything at all between sunset and sunrise!" explained Nan. "If they can go a whole night without eating, they turn back into normal pigs. BUT that's not all. Now, this is VERY important … there's something else—"

But at that moment the screen started to go all scribbly, the sound cut out, and Nan's face faded in and out of focus.

"She's breaking up!" said Fred. "Nan, can you hear us? What's important?"

"Hold your Horlicks, Derrick! I *am* coming to

polo!" said Nan to a man in a bright flowery shirt behind her before she started breaking up again. "First … pigs … need … frozen…"

"Yep, it's frozen all right. The connection's gone." Fred sighed as the call dropped and the screen went blank.

"Fred, now we *know* how to defeat them, I think we need to stop the pigs eating TONIGHT!" I said.

"Nan said to wait—" said Fred.

"But she ALSO said they get bigger when they eat! So what if they scoff LOADS tonight and get so enormous that even Nan won't be able to stop them! For all we know, Celery is off buying them more cakes!" I said. "We have to figure out how to stop their midnight feasting before it's too late. What do *you* think, Lily?"

I turned to see Lily with three sweet wrappers on the floor next to her. "*Gnaor, gnoar, arrrr, eeeearrr*," she said, nodding.

Fred picked up the wrappers. "Lily's been at the secret sweet stash while we've been talking to Nan. She's had three big toffees!"

"Lily! You'll be chewing for ages!"

"*Gnaoooooor!*" said Lily, her jaws totally stuck together with the toffee.

"Wait – that's it!" said Fred. "Toffee!"

"We know it's toffee, Fred. That's why she can't open her—" Then I realized what Fred meant! "She can't open her mouth!"

"If I can make some SUPER-sticky toffee to feed to the **zombie pigs**, then they won't be able to open their mouths for ages!" said Fred excitedly. "Maybe even an entire night…"

"And if they can't eat all night, they'll stop

growing and turn back into normal pigs!" I said, punching the air in celebration. "Let's do it!"

"But wait," said Fred. "What about the other 'important' thing Nan was about to tell us?"

I shook my head. "She was probably just going to say be careful or something! Grown-ups love saying that."

"In that case, I have some super-sticky toffee to make!" said Fred, pulling a couple of extra-shiny spatulas out of a crate.

Now we just needed to get Fred's toffee into the mouths of those **zombie pigs** before sunset...

CHAPTER NINETEEN

A very sticky steam fair

One thing you should know about people who live in the countryside is this: they love **steam**. Especially if it comes out of olden-day farm equipment. In fact, they love it so much they even have whole fairs about it! And as we found out from Mr Tibble, the parish council had organized one in our village later that afternoon.

Although, if you ask me, you should NOT call something a "fair" unless it has a roller coaster, a big wheel and candyfloss. Otherwise, people (me and Lily) will be very disappointed to find it's just a bunch of old tractor things!

Now, you might be wondering why I went to such a boring old event in the first place, especially in the middle of a zombie pig emergency. Well, guess what! The **Knobbly Bottom** Steam Fair was being held in the orchard next to Snoots' Farm, aka the **Zombie Pigs'** Lair! So me and Fred thought this would be the perfect chance to get the extra-sticky toffee to the pigs.

First, me and Lily spent the rest of the morning being super good and trying to convince Mum that going to a steam fair in the fresh air would be better for us than being stuck in the house doing three-hour musicals. I even made her some lunch (peanut butter on toast) and promised not to bake ketchup cakes ever again. Meanwhile, Fred persuaded Mr Tibble to let him cook again after our ketchup cake disaster (by blaming ME for all the mess!) and got to work making the stickiest toffee recipe in history.

So later that afternoon we met Fred in the back garden and stuffed as much of his **Extra-Sticky Toffee** as we could into our rucksacks and pockets.

The steam fair was even more BORING than I had expected. There were about five or six olden-day farmy things with steam coming out of them and a tea-and-coffee stall.

We told my mum that we were going to have a closer look at some tractors, then snuck off to Snoots' Farm to save the world.

BUT the problem with top-secret toffee missions is this: you might end up in a very sticky situation!

The first thing we noticed when we got to the giant pigsty was how quiet it was. There was no grunting or munching coming from inside at all.

Now, I would love to tell you that the **zombie pigs** had given up on their evil eating plan and had run off to live on a desert island, but that would be a LIE. The reason it was so quiet was because those gruesome greedos were asleep! We peeped through the window and saw them snoring away on the huge piles of stinky rubbish.

"They must get so tired from eating all night that they fall asleep in the afternoon!" said Fred.

"Great! Let's sneak the toffee into their feeding troughs before they wake up!" I replied.

But we were just about to creep over to the door when we heard a strange snuffling sound coming from inside.

Sniffle, snuffle, sniffle…

Were the **zombie pigs** waking up?

CHAPTER TWENTY

Let sleeping zombie pigs lie

At that point we decided the best thing to do would be to **GET OUT OF THERE**. But after the snuffling sound, a loud sob filled the air... A sob that didn't sound anything like a zombie pig at all. It sounded very much like a human crying! Was somebody in trouble?

"*Waa, wa, waaa!*"

When I peeked through the window, I couldn't believe who the secret snuffler was – CELERY SNOOT! She was putting food in the pigs' feeding troughs with tears streaming down her cheeks.

"What's wrong with Celery?" whispered Fred, as we watched her head to the pigsty door.

"Let's find out what she's up to once and for all!" I said, grabbing Fred and dragging him round the corner.

Celery was slumped on the grass outside the pigsty with her head in her hands.

"Celery Snoot!" I said, stepping towards her with my arms folded. "I think it's about time you told us what's going on with your pigs!"

Celery jumped and looked up at us in surprise. "What are YOU doing here?"

"We know about your pigs, Celery! They've been feasting on practically everything in **Knobbly Bottom**!" I said.

Celery buried her head in her hands again. "I know! But it wasn't my fault!"

"It's OK, Celery," said Fred, putting a hand on her shoulder. "We can help. Just tell us what happened."

"It's all gone wrong!" she cried, bursting into tears again. "My poor piggies have turned into horrid hungry hogs, and I don't know what to do! I just wanted to win the Golden Grunt!"

"What the heckedy-doo-dah is the Golden Grunt?" I asked.

And then Celery told us EVERYTHING.

Now, unless you're a PIG FARMER, you've probably never heard of the Golden Grunt. It's a bit like the dog show Crufts but for pigs, where they strut about fields like models on catwalks. And get this! The biggest, **PLUMPEST** pig of all wins the prestigious Golden Grunt Prize and ten thousand pounds!

Apparently, the Snoots' pigs always win, BUT last year a farmer called Swilly Whistle took home the prize! Now, one thing you should know about Celery Snoot is that she HATES losing pig competitions, and so she was determined to do everything she could to make sure she won this year – including feeding up her pigs as much as she could!

"When I fed them the apples from the orchard, I noticed that the more they ate, the bigger they got," said Celery. "But then things got out of hand! I don't know why, but the pigs *kept* growing AND turning *green*, and suddenly they weren't their cuddly cute selves any more. Now all they do is grunt at me for more and more food. But nothing fills them up! They are **INSANELY HUNGRY ALL THE TIME.**"

"Does your dad know about this?" asked Fred.

"No! If he finds out what I've done to his prize pigs he'll be so cross!" said Celery, sobbing again. "So I've been hiding them in here, but they're more out of control than ever. They've been venturing out at night and stealing food! I tried locking the pigsty, but they even chomped through the lock! Thankfully, they sleep for most of the day or they'd never stop eating!"

I frowned. "Wait. If your pigs sleep in the day and eat all night, WHO took my chocolate cake and picnic?"

"That was me, I'm afraid…" Celery sighed. "I had already given them everything in my kitchen, yet they were snorting for more! I had no choice but to take whatever I could find to feed them with."

"Including my hot cross buns!" I said.

"No, those were for me, actually," said Celery. "And I didn't *steal* them; I just got there first! But anyway, the worst thing is, I can't enter my pigs into the Golden Grunt like this!"

Fred stared at Celery in disbelief. "That REALLY *isn't* the worst thing, Celery! The worst thing is that you have turned your pigs into big green eating machines!"

Then Celery started crying again, so even though she was a blimming bun stealer, I felt a bit sorry for her.

"Look," I said, smiling at Celery, "don't worry. Lucky for you, we know how to fix your pigs, don't we, Fred?"

"Really?" said Celery, wiping her eyes on her sleeve. "How?"

"We have to stop them eating for a whole night!" explained Fred, opening his rucksack. "Luckily, I have prepared some super-sticky toffee that will glue their teeth together and stop them munching!"

"How do you know so much about my pigs and ... er ... toffee?" asked Celery.

Now, at this point I had to do a little tiny LIE

because we PROMISED Nan that we would never tell anyone the big scary secret about **Beastopia**. SO I told Celery there was a Perfectly Logical Explanation, and we'd found out that the apples in the orchard had been accidentally infected with *green radiation,* like what happened to the Incredible Hulk.

"Unfortunately, your pigs are now Incredible Bulks!" I said.

"But don't worry," said Fred. "The twenty-second rule of army training: always have something sticky up your sleeve! This toffee will sort them out."

"Are you sure?" asked Celery. "Have you actually tested it?"

"Not exactly," said Fred, "but it is at least one hundred and forty times stickier than my ordinary toffee, which takes exactly five point two minutes to chew. So I have calculated that this batch should keep their jaws shut tight for an entire night."

"It HAS to work!" I nodded. "What time do the pigs usually wake up?"

"Not until dinner time," said Celery, "and they always wake up grumpy, hot and hungry, so I leave them food and water while they're still asleep and get out of the way."

"Yes, I bet they are sweating like pigs in this heat!" I said.

"Well, actually, Maggie, did you know that pigs *can't* sweat? That is why they get so stressed in the hot weather, because the poor things can't cool down," explained Celery. "I know everything about pigs. Did you also know that they're scared of dogs, they don't like onions, and—"

"Look, all we really need to know is: do they like toffee?" I asked.

"Oh yes, they have a very sweet tooth," said Celery.

"Great!" Fred smiled. "If they eat the toffee when they wake up, it should lock their jaws shut until after sunrise."

"Are you sure they'll stay asleep all day?" I asked. "If they eat too early, the stickiness might wear off before morning."

Celery nodded. "As long as no one wakes them up."

"Well, let's get to work!" I said, and we snuck into the pigsty with our bags of toffee.

It was extra hot and smelly in there as the sun had been shining all day, making the rotten rubbish even stinkier! We tiptoed in and poured the sticky sweets into the sleeping pigs' feeding troughs like SILENT SNEAKY SANTAS, and those snoozing snorters didn't even stir!

BUT a few minutes later, something very noisy came hurtling through the door and ruined **EVERYTHING!**

CHAPTER TWENTY-ONE

The big toffee pig out goes wrong

"SUPER LILY TO THE RESCUE!" shouted my very noisy little sister at the top of her voice as she skidded into the middle of the pigsty in her tea-towel cape.

Me, Celery and Fred all went "SHHHHHHH!" at the same time, ducking behind some rubbish, but it was too late. The **zombie pigs** started to stir...

They twitched...

Then they yawned...

And then they opened their big green eyes!

THE ZOMBIE PIGS WERE AWAKE.

THE ZOMBIE PIGS WERE HUNGRY.

"Uh-oh!" I said.

They got to their feet – **Swinetta** and **Hogroll** on their hind legs and the rest of the swarm on all fours – and sniffed the air hungrily. Immediately, they spotted Lily, aka THE GIRL WHO HAD WOKEN THEM UP FROM A LOVELY SLEEP, and oinked angrily in her direction.

"GET OUT OF HERE!" I shouted to Lily as the **zombie pigs** took a step towards her.

"You don't have to tell me twice!" said Celery, who rushed towards the entrance.

"I was talking to Lily!" I shouted, just as that scaredy Celery disappeared out through the door.

Swinetta and **Hogroll** licked their lips and stomped towards Lily, followed by at least eight of the smaller **zombie pigs**. I would have to distract them!

Quickly, I grabbed a hard, stale half-eaten sandwich and clambered on top of a pile of rotten rubbish.

"EAT MY CRUST!" I yelled as I HURLED that stinky sarnie across the pigsty, and it bopped **Hogroll** on the head.

"OI!" squealed **Hogroll**, rubbing his head with his trotter.

"LILY, RUN!" I yelled, and made to race towards her, but **Swinetta** stepped towards me, looking really BIG, MEAN AND GREEN. I slipped in shock and rolled right down the pile of sloppy rubbish, landing near the huge hog's trotters.

"Nice trip, babes?" **Swinetta** grinned, straightening her tiara.

Fred ran towards Lily, but the other pigs surrounded him and bared their big brown teeth.

"RUN!" I screamed, as I tried to stand up in the skiddy scum pile, **Swinetta** looming over me. "LILY, WHY AREN'T YOU MOVING?"

"Ssssss-st-t-tuck," stuttered Lily, pointing to her feet.

That's when I realized. She had stepped in a big piece of extra-sticky toffee that had started to melt in the hot pigsty, and it had **GLUED** her to the floor!

I tried to drag myself across the slippery slope of waste towards Lily, but **Swinetta** reached down and grabbed my foot. *I had to do something before I became a pig's dinner!*

Swinetta was dragging me through the rubbish towards her when, luckily, I spotted a massive square of toffee on the floor next to me. I grabbed it and shoved it right into that pig princess's manky mouth!

I managed to wriggle away but watched in HORROR as **Hogroll** edged closer to Lily.

He smiled hungrily. "I fancy some human-beans on toast for my tea!"

Across the pigsty, Fred quickly picked up a piece of toffee, threw it up in the air like a tennis ball and BATTED it with his spatula – right into **Hogroll's** mouth!

"Mm, yummmm!" **Hogroll** grinned, and as the sweet, creamy flavour filled his mouth, he seemed to forget all about Lily.

Meanwhile, **Swinetta** squealed in delight as she chewed on the tasty toffee I had lobbed into her gob, and soon all the other pigs were wolfing down the treats we'd left in the troughs – not realizing that it would stick their mouths shut!

As soon as those greedy gut-stuffers were distracted, me and Fred rushed over to Lily. Taking one hand each, we *yanked* her off the toffee puddle – then we RAN right out of that disgusting den as fast as we could and slammed the door behind us.

We could hear the pigs oinking happily inside as they chewed on the delicious toffee. Hopefully, it would keep them busy for a while.

Fred frowned and checked his watch. "They ate earlier than we planned. There's a chance they'll be able to open their mouths again BEFORE sunrise."

Just then we spotted Celery heading back towards us, heaving her wheelbarrow.

"Onions!" said Celery. "Pigs cannot stand them!

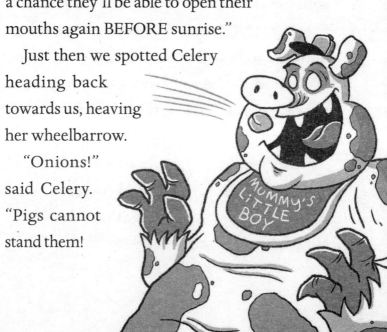

I thought if we pile these up outside the door, they'll take one sniff and stay inside!"

"It's worth a try," I said, and me, Celery, Fred and Lily started grabbing big brown onions from the wheelbarrow and heaping them outside the door of the pigsty.

After we had finished, we flopped down on the grass, exhausted, and crossed all our fingers and toes that the plan would work.

But then we had another sticky situation to deal with. And this one had *nothing* to do with toffee...

"LILY AND MAGGIE MCKAY!" yelled my mum, marching across the field towards us. "What have I told you about wandering off on your own? And look at the state of you both! What have you been doing?"

"Celery was just ... showing us her pigs!" I said, looking down at my dirty, slop-covered clothes.

"Well, how come Celery is nice and clean, Maggie?" said my mum.

"I like to make sure I set a good example for my pigs," said Celery smugly. "Do you know pigs are extremely clean animals?"

"Really?" said my mum, sounding quite surprised because of the disgusting stench drifting out of the pigsty. "Maggie, you are going *straight* home and into the bath. You were already in big trouble for making a mess in Mr Tibble's kitchen. I am NOT impressed!"

If I hadn't been SWORN to secrecy about **Beastopia**, I would have told my mum right there in front of Celery that it is NOT possible to save the world from evil beasts and stay clean! And I knew for a fact that Batman didn't have to wash his hair after defeating baddies. It was so unfair.

So I just STORMED OFF all the way home, which was actually really tiring, but you can't just STORM OFF halfway home. That would just be a SLIGHT BREEZE OFF, and I was more annoyed than that!

I really *hoped* that after all this, the pigs would be back to normal by morning.

But the next day we discovered that to defeat a swarm of **zombie pigs**, you needed much more than hope, toffee and a few onions...

CHAPTER TWENTY-TWO

Hell breaks loose before breakfast

The next morning, ALL HELL BROKE LOOSE! Now, if you live anywhere other than **Knobbly Bottom**, I expect you have no idea what hell breaking loose looks like. Well, it is a bit like this:

A STEP-BY-STEP GUIDE TO HELL BREAKING LOOSE

1. Your mum wakes you up extra EARLY to tell you that something terrible has happened.

2. You hide under the covers and try to go back to sleep because LAST time she said something terrible had happened it was just that she had run out of coffee. Then she made us

all go on an "urgent" early-morning trip to the shop.

3. Your mum then pulls the covers off you and tells you ALL HELL HAS BROKEN LOOSE in the village.

4. You look out of the window expecting to see DEMONS and MONSTERS and the DEVIL KICKING CATS, but what you actually see is that three of the garden chairs have fallen over and the back fence has been broken a bit.

5. But then your mum tells you to come and look out of the front door (where things are even worse) and you see the whole entire street IS a mess! Gates have been ripped off hinges, trees have been pulled out of the ground, and flower beds have been destroyed.

According to my mum, everyone thinks that Hell Breaking Loose was caused by a FREAK TORNADO during the night. As well as the mess along our street, half of a picnic bench, a third of a swing and the village hall entrance had all gone missing!

All our neighbours were out trying to clear up in their dressing gowns.

I spotted Fred and Mr Tibble on the green and ran over to them. Fred told me Jeffrey's kennel had been broken in half, Mr Tibble's barbecue had disappeared, and two of the greenhouse windows were smashed.

"Are you sure it was a tornado?" I said, wondering about a certain horde of horrid hogs with an appetite for destruction (and everything else).

Just then, the sound of a loud engine echoed across the green. We looked up to see a bright pink camper van with yellow stripes trundling down the little lane beside our cottages. The driver beeped a jolly-sounding horn as it pulled up outside Fred's house.

Then they slowly wound down the window and peered out at us from behind huge purple sunglasses.

"Hello, duckalucks!" It was Nan Helsing, still wearing her floppy sunhat. "What the helter skelter is going on here, then?"

"I'm afraid you've come back to a spot of bother, Nan! There was a tornado last night, and it made a right old mess of the place," said Mr Tibble. "I bet you are desperate for a cuppa after your flight. I'll stick the kettle on."

Then Fred and Mr Tibble invited me over for breakfast, so while Mr Tibble was making us tea and toast, we took the chance to tell Nan all about **Operation Toffee**. She sat in a big armchair, listening and sucking on a big red lollipop.

"So we MAY have stopped the **zombie pigs**!" I said. "We just need to get over to Snoots' Farm

as soon as possible to find out for sure."

"So you brainfreezled them too, then?" said Nan, suddenly looking very serious.

"Wh-what?" I stuttered.

"Brain freeze! You did hear what I said on the call, didn't you?" said Nan.

Fred and I looked at each other, then shook our heads.

"The video sort of cut out…" Fred muttered.

"Oh, bum chunks!" said Nan. "Big bum chunks with bobble hats on. You can't banish those beasts without giving them the brain freeze."

"Brain freeze?" I said. "Isn't that when you eat something sooo cold it gives you a headache?"

"It sure is, kidlings," said Nan. "See, to defeat a zombie pig, you have to do two things. Give 'em brain freeze, then stop 'em eating between sunset and sunrise."

"Uh-oh!" I said.

"The brain is the zombie's weak spot, and

the cold FREEZES their zombie powers, see. Obvious if you thunk about it!" explained Nan.

"Not to us!" said Fred.

"But we did work out to go for the brain!" I told Nan proudly. "We gave them a heavy-metal headache!"

"Not a bad attempt, kidlings – any headache will weaken 'em, but brain freeze is the only way to snuff that bad magic out from the inside!"

"So you're saying they must still be **ZOMBIES!**" groaned Fred.

Just then, Mr Tibble came in with a tray of tea and hot buttery toast, and a big frown on his face.

"This tornado has caused a lot of bother." He sighed. "Apparently, it broke Snaffle Snoot's pigsty door clean off! All his prize pigs have scarpered!"

As Mr Tibble went back to the kitchen to fetch some jam, Nan took the lollipop out of her mouth and looked over at us. "I bet my bottom knobble that there was no tornado," she said. "I think those pigs got out of the pigsty and feasted on the village while everyone was a-snoozling!"

"I knew it! They've gone on another hungry rampage!" I breathed out heavily. "Onions were obviously not enough to stop **zombie pigs**."

"Which means they'll have grown even bigger!" cried Fred.

"I wonder where they are now," I said. "If the pigsty is ruined, they'll have had to find another hideout to sleep in."

"Right," said Nan, gulping down her tea, "I'm off to get some ice cream."

Now before you say, "Why on earth does Nan Helsing, professional beast hunter, want ice cream at a time like this?" don't worry…

"Them pigs must be roasting in this heat. I say we cool 'em right down with a bit of brain-freezing ice cream!" smiled Nan.

Then she explained how we would defeat those petrifying porkers once and for all.

HOW TO DEFEAT ZOMBIE PIGS

1. Use extra-cold ice cream out of Gary's big freezers to FREEZE their brains.
2. Lure them to a church. (Everyone knows that evil creatures are VERY allergic to holy water and stuff, so baddies from Beastopia can't eat churches or anything in them! Apparently, Bibles taste like bogeys and Brussels sprouts – YUCK!)
3. Lock them inside the church until sunrise.
4. Have a sleep while the pigs' zombie powers disappear.
5. Let the pigs out of the church and eat a whole packet of Jammie Dodgers to celebrate that they are completely back to normal and we are HEROES!

But there was just one problem. We still had to find the **zombie pigs**!

CHAPTER TWENTY-THREE

A palace fit for a pig

After Nan left to find Gary and his two freezers full of ice cream, me and Fred took Jeffrey for a walk around the green but took a *slight* detour to Snoots' Farm.

We didn't tell my mum that bit, though, because mums do NOT like you taking detours across the village on your own. Now, before you say, *"Oh, Maggie, you told a dirty great lie, you must have pants FULL of fire!"* then listen to this! First of all, *technically* we DID go around the green with Jeffrey (we just went the VERY LONG WAY) and secondly, a teeny-tiny not-quite-the-whole-truth is OK if you are SAVING THE WORLD from evil beasts, so there.

If we were going to find out where those pigs

were, we needed to see if they had left a trail from their old lair! So Fred put two bottles of ketchup in his utility belt, I grabbed a handful of leftover extra-sticky toffees, and we headed across the green, along the footpath and through the orchard to Snoots' Farm with Jeffrey.

Broken branches and litter were scattered everywhere from the "tornado" (aka **zombie pigs**' midnight feast), but finally we made it to the pigsty. The door had been ripped off its hinges, and Jeffrey sniffed around the brown onions that had been trampled into the grass.

"Look for any trotter prints!" said Fred, inspecting the grass. But we didn't need prints. All along the field behind the pigsty was a trail of chewed-up EVERYTHING: bitten bushes, half-eaten sticks and a gobbled gate! It led to the garden of a red-brick farmhouse. "The pigs must be in there!" I said, pointing at the huge building.

Fred looked worried. "That's the Snoots' place! We should go and get Nan," he said, but Jeffrey had already started following the trail.

"There's no time!" I argued, grabbing a bottle of tomato ketchup out of Fred's utility belt. "We have to go and help them NOW!"

Fred nodded, and we followed Jeffrey across the field and through the chewed-up gate into the Snoots' garden.

The unusual red farmhouse was surrounded by hedges shaped like PIGS, and there was a PIG fountain with water squirting out of its snout, and a PIG-shaped statue on the lawn. There was even a PIG door knocker. It really was a **Pig Palace**!

The front door was wide open, but the garden was strangely quiet... Celery, Snaffle and the pigs were nowhere to be seen. *Had those ravenous runts scoffed the Snoots and scarpered?*

"Hello?" I hissed.

Suddenly there was a rustling sound from

behind one of the pig-shaped bushes. Then Celery and Snaffle Snoot crept out from behind it, looking very worried.

"Celery! Mr Snoot!" said Fred. "Are you OK? We, uh, came to check on you after the tornado!"

"Well, we appear to be in a bit of a piggy pickle," Snaffle said.

"I went to check on the pigs this morning, but they had gone!" cried Celery. "So Daddy and I searched for HOURS, then we just got home to find them asleep in our house! They're sprawled across the floor, the sofa – even in the bath!"

"Our poor pigs appear to have come down with some sort of swine fever," said Snaffle Snoot. "They're terribly bloated and green. I've never seen anything like it!"

"Yes, my darlings are suddenly sick," said Celery, shooting me a pleading look as she pretended to know nothing!

"I took one look at them and thought we'd best stay out here in case they are contagious," said Snaffle. "I was just about to call the vet."

"Um, don't do that!" said Fred. "We need to get Nan Helsing. She'll know what to do!"

"Really?" said Snaffle. "The little old lady from Knobs Hill?"

"Er, yes," I assured him. "See, we think your pigs managed to accidentally eat some radioactive apples. Nan comes from a family of er … *specialist* vets. She'll know exactly what to do."

"Good grief! Come on then, my sweet sourdough. Let's go," said Snaffle, taking an anxious-looking Celery's hand and jumping in the truck that was parked up by the gate. "You chaps keep an eye on my precious pigs, and we'll go and call on Nan Helsing!"

Then, just as Celery and Snaffle sped off down the road, something really *terrible* happened.

Jeffrey had spotted the open farmhouse door,

and he got all excited about somewhere new to explore! He ran towards it so quickly that Fred accidentally dropped his lead – and before we knew it, Jeffrey had shot inside the Snoots' house!

"Come back, Jeffrey!" yelled Fred.

Just when we thought things could NOT get any worse than a small Yorkshire terrier wandering into a house full of giant sleeping **zombie pigs**, Jeffrey started barking *really loudly*.

"Oh no!" I said to Fred. "Jeffrey is going to wake them up!"

"They might eat him!" Fred replied in horror.

All of a sudden, we heard some strange snorting noises coming from inside the house. Then we heard some shuffling and shaky-sounding grunting before those big green beasts piled out of the house looking **PETRIFIED**. Jeffrey had woken up the pigs, but they weren't eating him – they were running away from him!

"It's Jeffrey!" I said. "I had totally forgotten that Celery told us pigs are scared of dogs!"

One by one, those gigantic swine raced out of the front door and into the hot sunshine, squealing in terror, their eyes wide, as if they were running from a twenty-foot monster, not a teeny terrier!

Meanwhile, Jeffrey sat in the doorway, wagging his tail and looking very pleased with himself.

But there were two people on that farm who were not pleased with themselves. Two people clutching tomato ketchup bottles for dear life as a swarm of tired, hungry, startled **zombie pigs** headed right for them!

You have probably already guessed that those people were: ME AND FRED.

CHAPTER TWENTY-FOUR

Kiddy in the middle

Jeffrey had grown bored of the pigs and disappeared inside the house to find something more exciting to sniff, so the pigs weren't scared any more. Now, they were just ANGRY that they had been woken from their lovely sleep in the comfy, cool farmhouse.

The hateful horde looked straight ahead at us and snarled hungrily...

"Are you ready, Fred?" I yelled, holding my tomato-ketchup bottle up in front of me.

"Aim ... and fire!" he shouted.

Luckily, just as some of the drooling smaller pigs trudged towards us, Fred managed to squirt tomato ketchup into their mouths! Meanwhile, I pulled a piece of toffee from my pocket and threw it into the mouth of another. But they kept coming. We managed to hold off a few more, but there were still so many of them, dragging their zombie trotters towards us – including **Swinetta** and **Hogroll**!

The loathsome leaders ducked behind the smaller pigs every time we tried to hit them.

"I'm out of toffee!" I yelled to Fred.

"And the ketchup bottles are empty!" said Fred.

We had NOTHING left to slow them down!

Before we knew it, we were totally surrounded by swine. The smaller pigs circled behind us, and the pig princess and her scary sidekick stood in front of us.

"Who's for a game of kiddy in the middle?" **Swinetta** said to **Hogroll**, taking a step closer to us. "I don't know about you, but I'm feeling a bit peckish!"

"I'm always hungry!" growled **Hogroll**. "And I fancy a steak and KID pie!"

Just as we thought we were about to become
PIGSWILL, we heard a weird noise approaching
the farm… It was almost like a chorus of donkeys
trumping in a cave. It was so BAD I thought my
ears might actually be SICK!

Even the pigs stopped in their tracks and grunted in horror as the rotten racket got louder and louder.

"What *is* that?" I said, peering over the wall towards where the noise was coming from.

And there, on the horizon, we saw exactly what was hurting our ears. Mr Tibble and a group of about ten other people were heading our way ... and the trumping donkey sounds seemed to be coming from their MOUTHS!

"It's the **Knobbly Bottom** choir!" said Fred. "Also known as the WORST choir in the world!"

"They're SO bad," I said, clamping my hands to my ears. "What are they singing?"

"Some song from the olden days! BUT look at the **zombie pigs**!" said Fred, pointing to the animals that surrounded us.

They were lying on the floor with their trotters over their ears!

"The choir is giving them a headache!" I said. "Good old Mr Tibble!"

"Granddad, what are you doing here?" asked Fred, as we escaped the cowering pigs and ran over to the troupe.

"Old Snaffle is the choir master and we're supposed to be practising here tonight!" said

Mr Tibble. "What on earth is wrong with those pigs?"

"They're OK – just a bit of swine fever," said Fred quickly, as the pigs started to recover. "But can you sing again, please?"

"Oh, I don't know – Snaffle will be waiting for us. We were just warming up the old vocal chords on our way over," said Mr Tibble as the pigs started to stand up...

"Snaffle and Celery went out to get some medicine for the pigs," I said. "So please give us a little song – we were really enjoying it!"

Then, thankfully for the safety of the world (but not for our ears), Mr Tibble said, "Well, I suppose if Snaffle isn't home, we'll head back to the village – but we'll give you a little taster on our way out! A one, a two, a one, two, three, four..." And with that the choir burst into "song" again as they headed back towards the gate.

As their singing filled the garden, the **zombie pigs** looked horrified once more and stumbled about, trying to escape the awful sound. But before me and Fred could make a move, those grimy grunters came up with an idea!

Swinetta and **Hogroll** found a large compost heap at the end of the garden – and only went and put big clumps of sticky, soggy compost in their ears to block out the singing!

"OMG! Did you really think a crusty old choir would be enough to stop **Swinetta**?" grunted the petrifying pig, as the singers disappeared across the field. "Now, where were we, guys? Snack time?"

"YES!" cheered **Hogroll**, and all the other **zombie pigs** grunted greedily as their brains started to recover from the noise.

Me and Fred had just one choice: RUN as fast as we could towards the Snoots' front door. If we could get inside, we could lock ourselves in until Nan arrived!

But we didn't get far, because just as we reached the doorstep, that huge hulk **Swinetta** leapt across the garden and landed right in front of us!

CHAPTER TWENTY-FIVE

We all scream (and oink)
for ice cream

Have you even seen a **zombie pig's** tonsils?
Well, I have. That's how close I came to being a
swine's supper that day.

BUT luckily, just as **Swinetta** leant over me
and Fred, ready to swallow us whole, we were
saved by the bell – a loud dinging followed by
some cheerful music echoed across the farm.

Swinetta immediately turned to see where it
was coming from.

**Da da da da da da, da da da
da da daaaa…**

It sounded just like an…

"Ice-cream van!" said Fred, pointing to a
colourful vehicle hurtling towards the farm.

It was the weirdest ice-cream van I had ever seen. It looked more like someone had just painted **ICE-CREAM** on the side of a pink camper van. It had a big cardboard ice cream stuck to the front of it, and a huge speaker blaring out that familiar music everybody loves to hear.

But as the van got closer, I could see two people in white hats and aprons through the window. One looked very grumpy, and one had a lollipop hanging out of her mouth...

It was Nan Helsing and **Gary the Great and Evil Child-Eater**! They drove up through the gate and into the garden.

Luckily, Jeffrey chose this moment to finally come shooting out of the farmhouse, so as **Swinetta** backed away from him, I legged it over to Nan and Gary's van.

"Jump in, me duckalucks!" Nan said, and we didn't need asking twice. Fred grabbed Jeffrey, climbed into the van after me and slammed the door behind us.

"You OK, skiddiwinks?" asked Gary, ringing the bell and starting the engine. "Snaffle and Celery told us the pigs were here and we came straight over."

"Wait, where are we going?" I said to Gary. "Don't we need to give the pigs the ice cream?"

Nan smiled. "Not here!"

Then I peered through the window and noticed what those hot and hungry **zombie pigs** were doing! They sniffed the air and started plodding along behind the ice-cream camper van. It was like they were **hypnotized** by its music.

"ICE CREAM!" cheered **Swinetta**, scurrying after the camper van with her mouth watering.

"All oink for ice cream!" shouted Nan out of the window, and all the pigs grunted loudly and followed the camper van as it drove off the farm.

Nan Helsing was luring them away! She must have known *nobody* could resist an ice-cream van in a heatwave – not even an **evil zombie pig!**

"We need to get the pigs to the church – the one place they cannot gobble – and we'll brainfreezle them with Gary's extra-cold ice cream!" Nan explained, as a long line of **zombie pigs** trailed behind us. "Then we'll lock 'em

inside and *wham bam thank you, Nan*, they'll be
happy as normal pigs in mud by sunrise!"

A few minutes later Gary pulled up at the
churchyard, and the sweltering, starving swine
made their way over to us.

But the **zombie pigs** weren't the *only* ones who had heard the ice-cream van!

"Ice cream!" yelled Lily, running up to the van excitedly with my mum following close behind her.

"Double scoop of vanilla NOT cow-pat flavour ice cream with strawberry sauce, please!" Lily shouted up to Nan, who was leaning out of the window. Lily and my mum were so busy thinking about ice cream that they hadn't spotted the swarm of hungry **zombie pigs** heading up the road behind us!

"Maggie!" said my mum, spying me and Fred in the back of the van. "What on earth are you doing in there? You know full well you're not supposed to get into vans with *anyone*, even if they are full of ice cream!"

Behind my mum and Lily, the pigs were getting closer...

"Er ... remember those **zombie pigs** I told you about?" I said to my mum.

"Oh, Maggie, not more of your stories!" She sighed, but then a loud **GRUNT** made her jump out of her skin.

Mum slowly turned round to see the PIG PRINCESS herself, **Swinetta**, standing right behind her with her trotters on her hips!

"You OK, hun?" The huge hog monster smiled, as four smaller swine trudged over and stood behind her.

My mum's jaw dropped. Her face went completely pale, and I thought her eyeballs might fall out in absolute shock.

"Oh, you mean *these* **zombie pigs**?" squealed my mum.

"MUM, LILY, RUN!" I shouted, just as Nan slid open the van window. "Ice cream is on me, piggywigs!" she said, as she and Gary chucked boxes full of ice lollies and cartons of ice cream to the pigs.

Then Nan got out of the van and pulled a long cone-shaped gadget from her enormous handbag.

"Ice, ice, babies!" she yelled and began *firing* ice cubes into the zombies' mouths.

The scorching hot and hungry pigs could not believe their luck. They forgot all about Mum and Lily and RACED towards the cold ice creams with their tongues hanging out!

Now, have you ever seen a pig eat ice cream? Well, they eat it RIDICULOUSLY quickly. MUCH faster than humans who have skipped breakfast, or starving dogs, or even my friend Rav when he ate a whole bag of frozen peas in two minutes because he wanted to get his entire life's worth of five-a-day fruit or veg out of the way. (This was a genius idea if you ask me, but can you believe that when I asked my mum if I could eat six WHOLE tins of sweetcorn and then never have vegetables ever again, she said NO?)

Anyway, the **zombie pigs** ate so speedily that after a few minutes the whole pile of icy treats had gone!

But luckily for us, gobbling up cold food super quickly is the PERFECT recipe for brain freeze, and soon their headaches began to kick in!

The pigs stopped eating.

The pigs grimaced.

The pigs groaned.

Then they rubbed their massive heads with their trotters, and began stumbling around, moaning, bumping into each other...

Me and Fred took our chance. We jumped out of the van and ran over to join my mum and Lily, who were hiding behind a big oak tree.

That was when I made the mistake of saying, "THE PLAN IS WORKING!"

I REALLY should have known that as soon as heroes dare to THINK everything has gone RIGHT, something *always* goes wrong.

And something went wrong with a big fat cherry on top because, just then, we saw something terrifying heading down the hill towards the churchyard…

CHAPTER TWENTY-SIX

I wish pigs could fly right off and away from us

Can you guess what was clomping down the hill towards us?

I'll give you a clue.

It was HUGE, GREEN AND HUNGRY.

No, not the hungry caterpillar – MUCH bigger than that.

It was that horror **HOGROLL** – AND A LOAD MORE **ZOMBIE PIGS**!

"**Hogroll** has brought reinforcements! There must have been some deep sleepers left in the Snoots' house that Jeffrey didn't manage to wake up!" I said.

"What are we going to do?" Fred shouted over to Nan. "We're out of ice cream!"

"We've just had a shopping delivery, so I have a freezer full of frozen food?" suggested my mum.

"Granddad's freezer is full too," said Fred.

"Goodo, duckalucks!" said Nan. "Go and fetch the ammo, quick – we haven't got too long before the brain freeze wears off! Especially on the really big ones – they're so powerful they'll need more frozen fuel to stay weak!"

With one last look at **Hogroll** and the other **zombie pigs** trudging down the hill with their mouths wide open, me, my mum, Fred and Lily *ran* across the road to raid our freezers.

We managed to find two bags of frozen peas, nine choc ices, three burgers, a big box of fish fingers, potato waffles and a bag of chips. As we threw it all into bags, I told my mum EVERYTHING about the **zombie pigs**.

"And I moved to the countryside because I thought it would be SAFER than the city!" she groaned, putting her hair up in a Get Stuff Done Bun. She always puts her hair up when she has stuff to do: hoovering, washing up or slaying evil beasts! "Yet here we are about to be eaten by **ZOMBIE PIGS**!"

Now, I BET you have been waiting at least three pages for me to say this so GET READY, READER…

"I TOLD YOU SO!" I said to my mum, feeling very pleased with myself. "There are **zombie pigs** in **Knobbly Bottom**."

"No wonder the rent is so cheap," said my mum.

"I think what you mean is: 'I am sorry for not believing you, Maggie, and I'll never doubt anything you say EVER again!'"

Mum smiled. "Sorry, Maggie. I should have believed you," she said, giving me a big kiss on the top of my head. "So the sheep WERE vampires?"

"Yep," said me and Lily together.

"And the goblin rats that keep messing up your bedroom…?" my mum asked.

225

"Er … yes, definitely real," I said quickly. "But don't worry, we're beast hunters, and we have it all under control."

"I don't like the **zombie pigs**!" said Lily, looking a bit scared. "I want to stay here!"

"We can't leave you here on your own – you'll be safer with us," said my mum, taking Lily's hand.

"Come on, Lily, we need to get this frozen food to the church!" I said.

Lily shook her head firmly and folded her arms, like she does when my mum tells her she has to eat her vegetables. BUT luckily my mum has a very special power. She knows MAGIC tricks that get Lily to do stuff. Once she got her to eat THREE Brussels sprouts using a "spoon train" even though everyone knows trains are not made of spoon.

"Come on, love," said my mum. "Those **zombie pigs** are no match for the Fantastic Three. Plus, I have some jelly babies we can munch on the way."

Then we did our **Fantastic Three** high five! By the way, the **Fantastic Three** are a trio of FEARLESS heroes (aka me, Lily and my mum!) who can do ANYTHING, including saving the world from beasts and building really hard castles out of Lego.

After we had high-fived three times for luck, we grabbed our frozen treats and found Fred on the green with two more big bags of freezer food.

Together we ran back to the church as fast as we could – and it was *chaos*!

Unable to find any ice cream, **Hogroll** and the other pigs who hadn't been brain-freezed had begun munching everything in sight. **Hogroll** was chewing on a gate, another was scoffing a wing mirror, and two were fighting over the giant cardboard ice cream they had pulled off the van!

Mum pulled Lily safely behind a bush and grabbed a handful of fish fingers. "Right, let's save some bacon!"

I met her eye and nodded. Right away, I threw one of the big bags of frozen stuff over to Nan and Gary, and they swung into action, hurling it into the pigs' drooling mouths.

"Pig out on this, beast brain!" I shouted, throwing a handful of potato waffles into a pig's massive mouth.

"Get stuffed!" yelled Fred as he made a vanilla snowball from a family-sized tub of ice cream and batted it at another with his spatula.

Then, one by one, the pigs started to slow down, stumbling about the churchyard as they got brain freeze.

But just when I thought it was *actually* safe to say "THE PLAN IS WORKING", I realized there was one HUGE pig who we hadn't caught with our frozen missiles: **HOGROLL**. And he was right behind Fred!

"Fred, watch out!" I yelled.

Fred tried to get away, but he slipped in melted ice cream and fell to the ground.

My mum *dived* for one of the freezer bags. She fished around inside it and grabbed the very last piece of frozen food – an apple pie from Mr Tibble's freezer. She lifted it up in the air and aimed it at the pig…

"Wait!" I shouted. "That's one of Fred's apple pies! He made those with the apples from the orchard before we knew they had bad magic in them. If they eat THAT, they'll get even **MORE zombie powers!**"

Mum quickly chucked the apple pie into a bush instead. "We are all out of frozen food!" she yelled over to Nan and Gary, as **Hogroll** leant over Fred, mouth open.

"Not yet!" I said, whipping out a secret choc ice I'd stashed in my pocket. I looked at Fred. "Sixteenth rule of army training, right, Fred? Always carry a secret spare snack!"

Nan fired her ice-cube shooter at **Hogroll**. Unfortunately, he had his back to her, but she did manage to startle him by hitting him on the head! As he rolled on to the floor in shock, Fred managed to scramble away.

"How about a nice choc ice to cool you down?" I said, running over to **Hogroll** and holding the icy treat in front of his huge face.

"Mmm-mm!" **Hogroll** shook his sore head. "I saw what frozen things did to the others, and I ain't falling for it." Then he clamped his mouth shut. "Mm-mm."

"We need him to open his mouth!" said Fred.

"I've got an idea," I said, remembering my mum's magic spoon train. "Pass me one of your wooden spoons, Fred!"

Fred handed me a big wooden spoon from his belt, and I placed the choc ice on the end of it. Then I took a few steps towards **Hogroll**'s big head and lifted the spoon up into the air.

"Choo-choo! Here comes the train!" I said, moving the spoon right up to **Hogroll**'s mouth. "Choo-choo, choo-choo, open the tunnel!"

Then, just like Lily did with the Brussels

sprouts, as soon as the spoon reached that brute of a beast's lips, he could not help but open his mouth. Then I shoved the choc ice in!

His green face turned red with rage when he realized he'd been spoon-trained, but luckily the brain freeze kicked in and he rolled over and stumbled off across the grass.

"Well done, Maggie!" yelled Fred and my mum.

And so, FINALLY, every last one of those grotty **zombie pigs** was officially weakened with brain freeze!

"Time for the grand finale!" said Nan, putting her fingers to her mouth and doing a special loud whistle, which immediately woke up a snoozing Jeffrey. He shot out of the van looking excited and immediately started barking at the bumbling pigs. Terrified, they scurried away, looking for a way to escape.

"In here, piggies!" said Gary, herding them towards the church and opening the doors.

With Jeffrey's help, we all rounded the **zombies** into the church, and as soon as they were inside, Gary slammed the heavy doors shut and locked them with a big golden key.

"Well done, team!" Nan grinned, sticking a bright red lollipop in her mouth. "Now go and get some sleep, and tomorrow those little piggies will be right as rain."

Me and my mum ran to get Lily from behind the bush so we could do a celebratory **Fantastic Three** high five, but there was ONE big problem...

Lily was gone!

CHAPTER TWENTY-SEVEN

The biggest battle of all

"Maybe she ran home?" said Fred, searching around the churchyard.

Then suddenly a chilling, familiar voice came booming from above us.

"HEY, YOU GUUUUUUYS!"

We looked up, and guess who was sitting on the roof of the church and looking very smug… **Swinetta!** And she had grown to at least TEN FEET TALL (and when I say feet, I mean A GIANT'S feet because she was GINORMOUS). She looked a little woozy from the brain freeze, but still as TERRIFYING as ever.

But that was not even the WORST thing.

The worst thing was that sitting next to her up on the roof was LILY!

"Mummy! Maggie!" Lily yelled. "I want to come down!"

"But we're having so much fun up here," said **Swinetta**. "Although, I am starting to get very hungry."

"She's so BIG the brain freeze must have worn off already!" said Nan, staring up at the huge creature.

"Lily, do NOT move a muscle! I'm coming!" my mum yelled. Then she took a deep breath, ran forward and tried to actually CLIMB up a drainpipe that was running down the side of the church.

Now, because my mum isn't Spider-Man, I was NOT surprised to find that she couldn't climb up on to a church roof. Especially as she had rushed out of the house after the ice-cream van in her *fluffy slippers*. She tried and tried to pull herself up the thick black pipe, but she just kept slipping right down again.

"Epic fail, hun." **Swinetta** laughed above us. She adjusted her grubby tiara as she pulled off a roof tile and bit into it. "I stopped eating your ice-cold snacks when I realized what you were up to. How dare you try to weaken **Swinetta**? That's well rude, that is! I figure you lot owe me a FEAST fit for a princess. Or ... I might have to find something else to eat up here."

"I'm coming, Lily!" shouted my mum, having another go at climbing up to the roof but sliding down again. "Ugh, I knew I should have joined a gym!"

Just then, three roof tiles fell to the ground right next to us and Lily screamed.

"Help, Mummy!" cried Lily. "The roof is broken!"

"What are we going to do? None of us are big or strong enough to get up there and save Lily!" I cried.

"I'm scared, Mummy!" shouted Lily from the roof. "It's really high."

"Don't worry, Lily. I have a plan!" yelled my mum.

"Mum, what are you doing?" I shouted.

She was running over to the bush where she had thrown the frozen bad-apple pie. "I reckon to beat a **zombie**, you have to BE a **zombie**!" she said, as she picked up the defrosting pie and took two huge bites.

"MUM!" I screamed, but it was too late. She had swallowed the lot.

She looked at me with a determined expression on her face and sweat pouring from her forehead. Then she looked up at Lily on the roof and rolled up her sleeves.

"ROOOOOOOAAAAAAR!!" she shouted, before kicking off her fluffy slippers and *launching* herself at the drainpipe.

And can you believe that this time she managed to climb all the way to the top of that drainpipe without slipping and made it right up to the church roof?

Then she roared again, and grabbed Lily – just as a shocked **Swinetta** began to wobble, losing her balance on the broken tiles…

"Oi, princess pig face! Freeze!" hollered Nan, standing on top of the camper van and aiming her ice-cube shooter up at the baffled beast. *"Brain* freeze, that is. I gots you a refill."

And with the perfect aim of someone who has obviously been hunting evil beasts for years, she fired the last of the ice right into **Swinetta's** big mouth.

Then my mum gave one last mighty roar and shoved that **HUGE HOG MONSTER** right through the broken church roof!

There was a loud THUD as **Swinetta** landed inside the church, and my mum swiftly picked Lily up and slid safely back down the drainpipe.

"MUM! LILY!" I shouted. I ran over and gave her and Lily a big hug before remembering something REALLY important!

"We have to brain freeze you, quick!" I said to my mum.

But then I noticed something really strange.

My mum hadn't turned green! She wasn't even any bigger! She looked strangely … normal.

"Why don't you look like a **zombie**?" I asked her. "The pigs went green and grew bigger and stronger after eating the bad-magic apples."

"What do you mean?" said my mum. "I am stronger! Didn't you see me climb up that pipe after I ate Fred's pie? And I shoved that rotten swine through the hole in the church roof!"

"Wait, this is NOT one of mine!" said Fred, picking up the rest of the pie. "I threw all mine away after Lily ate one! This one's from the supermarket!"

"But ... how did you get super-strong **zombie** powers?" I asked my mum, staring at her in shock.

"Oh, I don't thinks it were **zombie** powers," said Nan knowingly. "I thinks she has superpowers of her own."

My mum smiled. "You might be right, Nan. I think when you become a mum you get a whole set of special powers!" she said. "So if your children are in danger, you not only get a bravery boost BUT super-strength too."

Nan winked. "The power was inside you all along, duckaluck!"

And then we all cheered – and you will be glad to know that this time, finally, NOTHING bad happened at all. That is, until Mr Tibble and his choir arrived at the church, singing at the top of their voices!

"Hello, me dears!" said Mr Tibble, looking around at the messy churchyard full of ice-cream wrappers, broken roof tiles and empty cartons. "We thought we'd practise at the church, but it looks like those foxes have been causing bother again."

Then we told the choir that the church was CLOSED for roof repairs, and Fred suggested to Mr Tibble that we all go home for a cup of tea instead. So we waved goodbye to the rest of the choir (who had thankfully stopped singing) and to Nan and Gary, who were staying in the camper van to keep an eye on the pigs overnight.

Nan said we should meet her at the church the next morning to see if the PLAN had worked. She also gave Celery and Snaffle a call and told them to come along at the crack of dawn to pick up their pigs, which she explained she had treated for "radiation-induced swine fever".

★

So, when morning came, we all gathered around and held our breath as Gary opened the big old church door...

For a few long seconds, everything was deadly silent.

And then... loads of very ordinary pink pigs came wandering out, looking very confused!

Celery ran over to them with tears in her eyes.

"Oh, my lickle piggies, you're all better!" she said, kissing them on the head, one by one.

"Bravo!" said Snaffle. "Thanks, Nan! I never realized we had a specialist vet in the village! But we really should report this radiation business to environmental health or the army, should we not?"

Nan, clearly an expert **Beastopia** secret keeper, answered without even hesitating. "Well, we could report it, Snaffle, BUT… didn't you and Celery want to enter your pigs into the Golden Grunt this year?"

"Yes! And we are going to WIN, aren't we, Daddy?" beamed Celery.

"Ah… Well, I heard they won't take any hog who has come into contact with radiation in case it has incredible hulked them up. It would be an unfair advantage, see…" explained Nan.

"Actually, thinking about it, probably best keep this to ourselves," stuttered Snaffle. "Our poor pigs have been through enough. The last thing they need is to be poked and investigated by health-inspector types. Best let them rest. Come on, Celery, let's get them back to the farm!"

CHAPTER TWENTY-EIGHT

The happy ending my mum ruined by saying I have to start school

So there you go. The **zombie pigs** were defeated and the secret of **Knobbly Bottom** was safe! Although, as my mum did actually help defeat the **zombie pigs**, Nan said it was OK to tell her all about **Beastopia**. Luckily, she agreed to keep it between us.

BUT the trouble with grown-ups is this: they don't want their children to live in a village that is home to an ancient evil magic because they think it's too dangerous. So she only went and said we should move back to Leicester!

But don't worry. Nan Helsing managed to assure her that the **Beastopian** magic would NOT rise to the surface again, because she and Gary had used some of Fred's super-sticky toffee to reseal the gateway underneath the big freezers.

Mum did join a gym, though. Just in case.

Nan said she is so tired she is going to "do nothing but Netflix" for at least two weeks, and after seeing how brave we were, Gary says he might even unban children from his shop.

Celery didn't win the Golden Grunt this year but says she will probably win the Bottom's Got Talent church-roof fundraiser instead (apparently she's taught her pigs the Macarena). Snaffle is organizing another **Poo Patrol** because the pigs left quite a mess, and as for me…

Well, even though I have saved the world from vampire sheep AND **zombie pigs**, my mum is STILL making me go to school in September! So, if evil beasts rise again and I'm too busy learning about fronted adverbials to save the world, it will be all my mum's fault.

Anyway, you probably won't hear from me

for a while because I'll be at boring old school.

Unless of course **Knobbly Bottom** Primary turns out to be as weird and exciting as the rest of the village...

I suppose we'll just have to wait and see.

THE END

But keep going for some extra material!

NAME: SWINETTA

SCARE FACTOR:	10
BRAVERY:	8
FIGHTING SKILLS:	8
NAUGHTY SCALE:	10

LIKES: Eating anything and everything.

DISLIKES: Tomato ketchup and being hungry.

SUPERPOWER: Can eat ANYTHING.

FUN FACT: Rubbish gives her bindigestion!

NAME: HOGROLL

SCARE FACTOR:	9
BRAVERY:	6
FIGHTING SKILLS:	7
NAUGHTY SCALE:	10

LIKES: Cake, cake and more cake.

DISLIKES: Tomato ketchup.

SUPERPOWER: Never feels full!

FUN FACT: Did a poo that was bigger than his head!

NAME: CELERY SNOOT

SCARE FACTOR:	3
BRAVERY:	5
FIGHTING SKILLS:	3
NAUGHTY SCALE:	8

LIKES: Pigs and hot cross buns.

DISLIKES: Losing the Golden Grunt Award.

SUPERPOWER: She knows 321 pig facts.

FUN FACT: She named her piglets Harry Trotter, Herswiney Granger and Ron Squealsy.

NAME: SNAFFLE SNOOT

SCARE FACTOR:	3
BRAVERY:	4
FIGHTING SKILLS:	1
NAUGHTY SCALE:	5

LIKES: Running the Poo Patrol.

DISLIKES: People who don't scoop their poop!

SUPERPOWER: He can tell what animal a poo belongs to by sniffing it.

FUN FACT: He sleeps with a fluffy toy pig!

Tomato-Ketchup Cupcakes

Do you dare to try them?

What you need:

240g plain flour

2 tsp baking powder

1 tsp bicarbonate of soda

2 tsp cinnamon

115g tomato ketchup

115ml water

2 tbsp red food colouring

170g butter, softened

300g brown sugar

2 eggs

Cream-cheese frosting (you can buy it from a shop or
    make your own using full-fat cream cheese, icing
    sugar and butter)

12 cupcake cases

**Note: Remember to ask a grown-up to help
you when you're using a hot oven.**

Method

1. Heat the oven to 180°C/160°C fan/gas mark 4.

2. Line a cupcake tray with 12 cupcake cases.

3. Mix together the flour, baking powder, bicarbonate of soda and cinnamon.

4. In a separate bowl, mix together the ketchup, water and food colouring.

5. In another bowl, beat together the butter and brown sugar until light and fluffy, then add the eggs one at a time.

6. Gradually add the flour mixture and the ketchup mixture to your butter, brown sugar and eggs, and mix well.

7. Scoop the mixture into the cupcake cases and bake for 15 minutes or until a skewer poked through the middle comes out clean.

8. With a grown-up's help, place the cakes on a wire rack and allow to cool completely.

9. Decorate them as you like with cream-cheese frosting!

10. Enjoy with your friends and family. (Avoid eating with zombie pigs unless you want a VERY smelly kitchen.)

Knobbly Bottom Beasts And How To Banish Them

The Helsings' guide to banishing all manner of evil and terrifying beasts

ZOMBIE PIGS

WHAT THE HECKERS ARE THEY?

A greedy bunch of beasts with creepy green eyes and dirty broken teeth who are always hungry. They gobble up everything and anything they can get their sloppy mouths on! But it gets worse… They grow BIGGER every time they EAT. This porky pack of beasts are led by the hideous Swinetta and her disgusting sidekick Hogroll.

ABILITIES

Unlike your average zombie, these greedy gut-stuffers are gigantic. So not only are they greedy but they are insanely strong too.

LIFE GOALS

They don't want to take over the world – they want to EAT it. They won't stop scoffing until they have eaten *everything*. Even you, me duckaluck.

LIKES

Food, food and more food. No – more food than that. Now multiply that by ten million. That's how greedy these piggies are.

DISLIKES

Ketchup, feeling hungry and brain freeze!

WEAKNESSES

Tomato ketchup slows them right down, as it gives those ravenous rascals a tummy ache. (Be warned: this results in VERY stinky wind!)

HOW TO BANISH THEM

The only way to turn them back into normal pigs is to do two things. First, you feed them enough ICE-COLD food to give them brain freeze. Then, once they are all freezled and stumbling about like wallies, you must STOP them from eating anything for an entire night. This is the ONLY way to rid the pig's brain of the bad zombie-making magic once and for all.

ACKNOWLEDGEMENTS

Writing a book takes a massive amount of teamwork and so I want to say a big fat thank you to all the Scholastic superwomen who helped me with my zombie pigs!

Firstly, thanks to my editor, Julia Sanderson, for her fantastic edits, advice, brain-freeze insights and patience. I quite literally could not have finished this book without you (and coffee). A HUGE thanks to the amazingly clever Wendy Shakespeare for your eagle-eye edits, Sarah Dutton for her expert schedule management, Harriet Dunlea for working so hard on organizing an epic book tour, and Hannah Griffiths for all things marketing. I am also so grateful to my fabulous agent, Anne Clark, for her unwavering support and guidance.

Thanks to Jeff Crowther for seeing into my brain and bringing Knobbly Bottom to life, and the designers for making the book look really cool!

I also couldn't have finished this book without the support (and childcare) of my family and friends. Thanks to my mum, dad and brother, James (happy now, bro!), for everything, and Laura, for her hilarious performance as Nan Helsing (and being the best sister ever).

Thank you to Poppy, Jackie and Emma, who have been such good friends through a tricky few months of juggling kids, life and writing. And huge thanks to my kick-ass HCWK crew – Laura, Emmaline and Tamsin for your love and inspiration, my gorgeous Scare Crows, Tony Award winner Caz for the roam moans, and Michael Cameron for your help with the public speaking and donkey trump puns.

I would also like to thank all the children who have read and laughed at my knobbly bottom! I have really enjoyed reading your reviews and seeing your pictures of scary beasts and even mock-up front covers!

And, finally, thank you to my extraordinary daughters, Isla and Cleo, for being so brilliant and always making me laugh. We will forever be the Fantastic Three.